April *To:*

Welcome Nanaism

Marie Rickwood

RULES FOR LIVING ON
EARTH

Marie E. Rickwood

Marie E. Rickwood

5536 Norton Rd.
Nanaimo, B.C.
Canada V9T 6S2

Home (250) 758-0121
Cell (250) 716 - 6727
~~halfcord@shaw.ca~~
marie rickwood @ shaw . ca

MW00982208

◆ FriesenPress

Suite 300 - 990 Fort St
Victoria, BC, V8V 3K2
Canada

www.friesenpress.com

ISBN
978-1-5255-2859-0 (Hardcover)
978-1-5255-2860-6 (Paperback)
978-1-5255-2861-3 (eBook)

1. FICTION, VISIONARY & METAPHYSICAL

Distributed to the trade by The Ingram Book Company

Table of Contents

This novel is dedicated to my children
and their spouses,
And to my grandchildren
and all future descendants.

Thank You

To my sons:

Rory Rickwood, UE, BA, CPHR, for his inspiration and for sharing our love of writing.

Derek Rickwood, BFA, and Master Painter for lending his gift of painting talent to create and paint Second Chance Theatre.

And to my son-in law:

Harvey Huebsch, P. Eng., for taking the time to read the manuscript and for offering words of encouragement.

To: Gordon W. Pascoe, originally from the Isles Of Scilly, off the southwestern tip of Cornwall, England. He wears many hats: retired school teacher, a composer, a musician, an actor, a theatre director and dancer. The beautiful creation of music in this novel is his Opus 106.

To: Bonnie Patterson, Natural Health Advocate for taking the time to critique the manuscript and for giving me her unlimited support.

Thank you to my editor, Donna Marie West of Montreal who so professionally shook all the wrinkles out of my blanket of words. Thank you Donna.

Appreciation is also extended to my dear neighbor, Iolanda Ghazé, a graduate of the Global Leadership College in Toronto, Ont. Iolanda helped me begin the writing journey of this novel.

A very special and heart-felt thank you to my husband, Val Fenton. His unending support and keen interest in my writing has been my ultimate inspiration.

Preface

Where do we go after we die? A few people have claimed after death experiences. Some have experienced a light at the end of a tunnel while others claim to have made it all the way to Heaven; from there they received wise and believable words of faith and returned to tell us.

However, it has been impossible for anyone to come back with definitive proof.

Consequently, we only have our Christian beliefs to answer the question of where we go after we die. The answer is the mystical place called, Heaven. We are promised we will go there if we obey God's commandments and think of Jesus as our Saviour.

However, we have more than our beliefs, we have our imagination. To use our imagination and to put it down on paper takes a certain amount of courage. Somehow it seems one who does, is forming a kind of sacrilege.

But shouldn't we have the right to write if we have been given a gift to do so?

And our reader must realize it is the writer's imagination of what this mystical place is, not a proven fact, however it might stimulate in others to go beyond what has been taught and imagine what might be.

This also applies to God the Father. Christians know who Jesus, the son of God is, because He lived and walked on earth and left an everlasting legacy. They have learned about the Holy Spirit despite the fact some may not realize they have personally encountered this part of the Trinity.

But to imagine what God might look like, whether God is female or male, whether His skin is black, white, yellow, or brown, or if in fact He has any skin at all triggers the imagination to go even further. And while the imagination is searching, scheming and praying to come to a conclusion, the fact remains the results will be only one person's imaginative concept.

This novel will take you through all of the above and hopefully will give you a new outlook and imagery of God the Father and this mystical place called, Heaven.

RULES FOR LIVING ON EARTH

1

Up

BEFORE I felt it, I saw it—a blinding, red pain exploding in every neuron in my brain. I tried to escape, but it travelled rapidly toward me and over me, grabbing, twisting, and grinding me down. I felt the rough texture of the pavement slam against my cheek with such a force I heard my cheekbone crack. Fused to this surface, I could smell burnt rubber and, for some strange reason, bubble gum. I managed to open one eye just a slit. An oil pump jack came into view. *Can't be*, I thought, *not here*. Of course not … it was merely a grasshopper. I realized this when it leaped up, crackled a hiss, and flew away, taking with it the last remnants of pain and all of the light.

In the darkness an accumulation of sound remained: a woman crying, a man's voice saying "Ah, the poor fella. I think I've seen him before in my bank," and a younger voice murmuring, "I wonder if he's dead." I heard the sound of a woman sobbing, and then a deep, teary voice whispered hoarsely in my ear.

"So sorry, man. I hit the brakes hard but couldn't stop the big rig. You stepped right out in front of me."

Above the drone of traffic, I could faintly hear the moaning of a siren before all seeped slowly away into silence.

My life on Earth had come to an end!

I felt weightless and began floating up, up until I found myself hovering. The scene below was mind-bending. I saw my broken body lying on the ground, being administered to by paramedics. I saw them desperately trying to revive me, and I wanted to shout, "Hey down there. You're wasting your time. It's too late; I'm dead."

It was as if they heard me, for at that moment they covered my body with a blanket, drawing a harmonized, "Ahhh!" from the large, curious crowd that had gathered. *I must have been important to command so much attention; perhaps I should be taking a bow.* That thought fleeted away like dissipating fog as the scene below shrunk smaller and smaller until disappearing altogether.

Having just had the vision of my body on the ground, I checked to see if I had another. And indeed I did—a large, phantom-like appendage floating behind me. I saw my Omega watch on my wrist that had so faithfully kept me on time for the many things in my life: boardroom meetings, sales meetings, doctor's appointments, air flights, meetings with my stockbroker and lawyer, and those clandestine meetings with my lady friend. But now the face of the Omega was vacant; time no longer held any significance.

Where's the light at the end of a tunnel I've heard people say they'd seen? Probably, I rationalized, they in fact had not really died like I'd just done, for if they had, they wouldn't be back to talk about it. Death is a final state—there's no return. The thought jarred my senses. My cognition was still very much intact. I thought of the family I'd left behind and imagined the state they would be in, and my throat constricted.

I kept soaring like a helium balloon in the wind. I could see the clouds parting before me as I flew through clouds of all colours in deep, shimmering hues of magenta, turquoise, and golden yellow. In the distance I could see a path forming. Instantly I was upon it, slowly walking—not by my own volition, but rather by some mysterious force I couldn't explain. A building came into view. It was black in colour with bright yellow, large double doors. The Star of David was emblazoned in the centre of each.

As I approached and made my way up the steps, these doors soundlessly swung open and a loud voice ordered, "Come in and sit down."

There were two chairs in the middle of a small, empty room. I sat on the nearest one and waited. All my life I'd welcomed a challenge, relished a new experience, but now fear engulfed me as I waited in unnerving silence. I tasted the salt of perspiration beading on my upper lip. I felt my heart thump against my rib cage like it wanted to escape. Clearly, my emotions had escaped death.

"Jonathan Brown, I wasn't expecting you so soon. What was your big hurry crossing the street? As a child you were taught to look both ways."

The owner of the voice, a robust, middle-aged man with an unruly thatch of white hair, appeared in the chair across from me. I hadn't seen him enter the room.

"I did look both ways," I replied in a voice that sounded strange to my ears.

"You looked to the left but not to the right, because if you had, you would've seen the truck and you wouldn't be here now, but that's all irrelevant. Let's get down to business."

He rubbed both hands together as if he was about to enjoy something.

"You have me at a disadvantage," I said. "You know my name, but I don't know yours. Who are you anyway?" There was unintended impertinence in my voice.

"You can call me the Agent, the Greeter, or even the Explainer. Yes, the Explainer is best, as I will be explaining things."

"Where in God's name am I?" I asked.

He just smiled, stood up, and said, "Let's get on with it, shall we? Follow me."

When he turned around I saw that he was wearing a skull cap. We left the small room and walked down a long, narrow corridor. The fear I'd been feeling was replaced with anxiousness. I could smell lilacs mixed with a faint smell of lemons, and I could hear a distant flute playing an unidentified melody. As I nervously pondered what lay ahead, I gazed down at his feet and then at mine. We seemed to be gliding rather than walking—strange bit of business.

Finally, we reached a much larger room that held an air of tranquillity. I was completely awestruck. Against the far wall were bright-red neon lights that made me squint. Beneath the lights were the words in large, black, capital letters:

RULES FOR LIVING ON EARTH

I tried reading the rules, but they faded away before I could, which frustrated me further. I wondered if it was deliberate.

The Explainer turned to me and said, "As you no doubt read, Jonathan, listed there on that wall are the rules for living on Earth. You were taught all of these as a child, just as you were taught to look both ways. We both know what happened with that bit of advice. Now that you've died, we need to see how you managed life's rules, one at a time. You will be visiting different stations; each will represent a rule, with five in total. Upon arrival, you will be met by someone who will guide you. You will start with the first station, and if you finish that one successfully, you will move on to the next one, etcetera, etcetera. But the last station, the very last station, will be the most important of all."

Naturally I wondered about the very last rule being the most important. Obviously he wanted to keep me guessing, and his singing out of the etceteras annoyed me. In fact, the whole scenario was annoying the hell out of me. Didn't he realize who he was dealing with? Didn't he know I was the president of one of Canada's largest financial institutions? I deserved some respect.

"Just a minute here … I demand some answers. Where am I? What am I doing here? Where am I going?" My voice was two octaves higher than normal.

The Explainer just smiled, like he was remembering some private joke.

"I want to speak to your boss!" I shouted.

He laughed aloud, held up his hands, and declared, "Jonathan, let's hope you make it that far. Patience was never one of your virtues—that was proven earlier when you unfortunately paid the consequence. There's more to explain, but seeing as you are in such a hurry, we can skip over it. Let's move on. In time, you will have your answers. Good luck, Jonathan."

Before I could respond, I felt the force once again move my feet across the room and out the door. I was alone with my frustration and thoughts. I didn't have to wait long, however, as another path appeared and slowly my feet were gliding along.

My frustration kept building as I slid at a snail's pace along this new path. *Why do they, whoever they are, move me along so slowly?* Although my body had expired, my memory of it made it feel like I still had it. My emotions and my mental perception were very much intact. In fact, I was forced to think about and contemplate my past and how those left behind on Earth would be reacting to my death. My wife, Gina, would be crying uncontrollably and needlessly worrying about finances. My girlfriend, Rosalyn, would be remembering our last tryst in her apartment, and my twin sons, both college students, would be desperately trying to console their mother.

And I was forced to think about what lay ahead. What was happening to me? What would I see? Who would I meet? And where the Sam hell was I headed?

I felt a mixture of remorse, fear, and anxiety all rolled up in a ball. All was painful, made more so by this inchworm-pace of movement forcing me to recollect my past life on Earth.

I glanced to my left and right and could see a faint outline of many people walking on many paths, duplicated in the way a series of mirrors would capture. I wondered if this whole process was the Catholic thing called Purgatory.

Finally, after what seemed an eternity of frustration and painful memories, another building appeared through the mist ahead of me. As I drew nearer, my interest peaked. I could see a large number 5, printed in

black on the white door of the simply constructed, one-storey building. The wise guy
who called himself the Explainer had said I
would begin with the Fifth Rule for Living
on Earth. It took forever to get there, but
finally I was propelled up the stairs and
through the open doorway. I found myself
in a room where two easy chairs were positioned in front of a large, white screen.
Printed in florescent green were the words:
DO NOT BE ENVIOUS OF YOUR FELLOW BEINGS.

An aroma of chocolate broadcasted the
entrance of an elderly gentleman with
shocking white hair. He was wiping his
hands on his white apron, leaving brown
smudges all over it.

"Hello, Jonathan," he said with famil-
iarity. "I've been preparing for your visit. There are four dozen chocolate cookies
in the oven. I know how you love chocolate. But first, come, sit down." He gestured to a chair, and I sat down. "We have
some talking to do. My name is Matthew."
Pointing at the screen, he proudly declared in a quivering voice, "I'm the man
in charge of the rule, Envy."

I noticed his hand had a slight tremor,
which I assumed was due to his age.

"Let's talk about what it means. First,
tell me how you would define envy. Please
give me your definition, Jonathan."

He raised his eyebrows inquisitively while his eyes bore into me like a laser. I had the sense he knew something about me—actually, a whole lot about me, much of which I didn't want to admit or, in fact, recollect. At least he was more direct than the Wise Guy. I thought the question was simple and easy to answer, so I quickly blurted, "Well, Matthew, my definition of envy is when you wish you had what someone else has."

The thought that my response pushed his question to the ridiculous filled me with pride.

"That's true, Jonathan, but we need to ask ourselves what happens when one is envious. What happens when the insecurity of jealousy joins forces with envy? What happens then, Jonathan?" His eyes bore into me again accusingly.

I had to turn away. *How am I supposed to have all of the answers to those philosophical questions? Ask me something about the corporate world, about investments, about how to have one's finger on the market's pulse, knowing when to buy low and sell high. Ask me how to show a profit when all odds are against it. How to choose the right staff; those things I can answer. But all of this crap about envy I'll leave to the psychologists. I* wanted to shout this to him, but instead I went on the defensive.

"I cannot say I've never been envious, Matthew. Sure, I've been envious at some time or another." This time I turned and met his gaze with assertive eyes. "So?"

"Yes, that's true, Jonathan, but nine times out of ten, the other beast joined in and weakened your moral character. No doubt you've heard the expression, "green with envy." However, when jealousy is added, it's far more appropriate to call it, "red" with envy … from that evil arises." His voice quavered.

He gave that piercing look again and I noticed his hands displaying a more greatly pronounced tremor. Once again, my defensive mode came to the fore.

"Well, I'll have you know, I've never been red with envy, as you put it." I gave him the "so there" nod.

Coupled with his yellowing teeth, a rueful smile was dancing amongst the wrinkles on Matthew's face, giving him a sinister appearance.

"I think it's time we explore your life and see firsthand how you handled this particular Rule for Living—how you handled envy, Jonathan. I'll be right back." He stood up slowly and, placing his hand on the small of his back, left the room hunched over.

Again it seemed like hours before he returned, but when he finally did, he was carrying a large tray of chocolate cookies, their aroma striking full force. I could feel my mouth watering. My eyes beaded on a DVD stuck in the bib of his apron, and I rationalized that was the reason for the big screen. I wondered what was next, what was on that DVD.

"Help yourself," he said, setting the tray down on the table between us. He reached into his bib and extracted the DVD. Aghast, I noticed the words printed on it: The Life of Jonathan Brown/Envy.

"Thank you," I muttered. Suddenly, I had no appetite.

My eyes were directed to the screen to see the same words forming in, of all colours, bright red. I sat dumbfounded in my chair. I could feel my heart quicken. Was I about to see my life enfold? The skeletons in my closet began rattling their bones at me like a sabre. I breathed deeply and settled back, engulfed with trepidation while the progressive, eerie sound of Johan Sebastian Bach's Toccata and Fugue in D Minor carried me back to Earth.

2

Busted

Fourteen-year-old Jonathan Brown bounced his fingers across the keyboard like he was dribbling a basketball, while bobbing his head in unison with the notes. At the conclusion of Bach's unnerving piece, he pushed his unruly, brown hair away from his eyes and gazed out the window.

Two officers from the Vancouver police department were walking around the neighbour's brand new, white Cadillac that was resting on its rims. The sight of them made his heart quicken. They looked so important, so strong. Jonathan felt frightened.

Oh, but they'll never know it was me. There was no one around. No one saw me. I'm safe.

As he sat pensively watching them walking around and inspecting the vehicle, his thoughts flew back to the time when his family moved to the Shaughnessy District of Vancouver in Canada's most westerly province, British Columbia. He was eight years old. His father had accepted a position at the University of British Columbia, leaving behind a teaching position in the interior. He recalled how excited he'd been about moving to Vancouver and into this big, white house with a basketball hoop at the rear of the garage. His delight with his new home had diminished instantly when he saw the house next door, however. It not only had a basketball hoop, but also a swimming pool and tennis court, with a parade of young boys coming and going. They dove into the pool one after the other, squealing with delight. He listened to their whooping and hollering and wished he had a yard like that with all of those friends. He wished it were him having all that fun. He wished he had a sibling, someone to share things with, to whisper to at the dinner table about how he hated green beans and fried onions. He couldn't tell his mother; that wouldn't be polite, since she'd prepared the dinner. Besides, complaining about the food just wasn't done … not at their table. His hopes of ever having a brother or sister had long since passed. His mother looked far too old to have a baby. He'd often seen his parents quietly talking together. They had each other. He had no one.

One of the boys living next door, Brent Halliday, after these past six years and to this day, had yet to acknowledge Jonathan's presence at school, nor across the fence in the back yard. His nose was always in the air like he was the Lord of the Rings.

Late in the afternoon of the previous day at the beginning of the summer holidays in 1989, jealousy had joined envy to tip the scales. Jonathan had been sitting on his front steps reading over his math textbook when a big, white Cadillac pulled up in front of Brent's home. Jonathan had released a slow whistle. Instantly, Brent and his younger brothers had come rushing out to greet their father.

All three boys had run around the car, peering into its interior, kicking its tires, and trying the doors.

"Hey, Dad, did you buy it?" Brent had shouted.

"Yup, it's ours." His father had stood back proudly, wearing a smile and obviously enjoying his sons' response.

"Really cool wheels, Dad, really cool!" they'd exclaimed.

"We have the best car on the block. I can't wait to ride in it," declared Brent.

When Brent had turned his head, Jonathan knew he had seen him, sitting there like a nerd with a textbook on his lap. Brent had put his chin up in the air and flipped him the bird. He may as well have also thumbed his nose at him. He was seething inside and felt a jealousy like no other. It was then that he'd felt a strong need to do something to the car, and a plan had slowly formulated with absolutely no thought to consequences.

He had waited in his room that night until two in the morning with hopes the car would still be on the street. A peek out the window had shown it was. He recalled noticing that their garage was being renovated, so the car could be on the street for a few days.

I'll fix that conceited pus head, he thought.

Jonathan had put a large red crayon in his pocket and quietly tiptoed out to his father's garage to take the needle-nose pliers from the tool box. With his heart thumping, he'd snuck around to the front of his house and to the street. There wasn't a soul in sight. He'd glanced at Brent's house and seen all of the curtains drawn and the lights out. He'd quickly run around the car and crayoned all of the windows, and with the pliers in hand, he'd let the air out of the two front tires. Then he'd proceeded to the back of the car where he repeated the process. Slowly the big car sank down to its rims with a quiet swoosh. He'd scurried back into the house and up to his room. Breathlessly, he'd returned the pliers to the tool box and put on his pyjamas and crawled into bed, wishing he could witness their reaction in the morning. All of this had been accomplished in less than five minutes.

The policemen left and walked up the street. Jonathan could see them ringing door bells. He turned back to his piano and, galloping his fingers across the keyboard to the notes from Beethoven's 5th, he totally captivated himself in the music and lost any concept of time.

Later when his mother entered the room and marched up to him, he wasn't aware of her until she spoke his name.

"Jonathan!"

One look at her told him she was angry.

"We know what you did to the Hallidays' car."

"I didn't do anything," he retorted, at the same time wondering how he'd been found out. Had he not checked carefully to see that no one was looking, and no one was on the street?

"What is it you think I've done?" He looked her square in the eye.

"You know very well what you've done. You cannot lie your way out of this one, Jonathan Brown. We know what happened. We're not raising you to be a criminal! What you did is despicable! How could you do such a thing?" His mother's voice was loud and shrill. "Your father works hard at the university to give you this life, this home, and this is how you repay him?"

She gestured wildly, sweeping her arm around the large living room with its high ceilings, Persian carpet, and grand piano sitting in the alcove amongst the tropical plants. A stack of classical music piled high on a mahogany table nearby was an indication of the many music lessons given to Jonathan.

"What do you have to say for yourself?"

Jonathan sat with his head down, quietly receiving the full force of his mother's anger, but it could not break through the armour he'd wrapped around himself.

How could she possibly know? She must be bluffing.

"I didn't do anything," he lied. "I didn't do anything!"

His mother threw up her hands. "Just wait 'til your father gets home. He'll deal with you." With tears of disappointment hanging on her eyelids, she quickly did an about-turn and left the room.

Jonathan sat there; he wasn't about to admit anything. They had no proof. Although he'd felt the sting of his mother's anger, it was his father's perceived discipline he was dreading. He would be home from work around 5:30 PM, just in time for dinner. Jonathan could smell roast beef cooking and felt hungry. He didn't want to miss out on dinner; his stomach was already growling.

He saw the policemen leave the Hallidays' house, get into their car, and pull away. He checked his watch. It was 5:15 PM. They'd been investigating nigh on two hours.

Dad should be home any minute now.

***

Professor Brown had worn a suit for the departmental meeting rather than his usual sweater and slacks. As Dean, he had to set the standard for deportment. It had been a long day and when he'd gotten into his car to drive home, he'd loosened his shirt and took off his tie. The aroma of roast beef was a comforting welcome when he stepped through the door; however, the sight of his wife, Jane, was not so pleasant. He could tell she'd been crying. The last thing he needed now was another problem; the day had been filled with trying to find resolutions. But something definitely was amiss on the home front. He gave Jane a quick peck on the cheek and stated,

"Pour us a drink; I'm headed upstairs to change."

When he returned to the kitchen he saw two glasses on the small table in the breakfast nook. Upon approaching, he could hear the ice still crackling in the drinks. Through the archway to the kitchen, his wife was busily finishing the last details of the dinner: Mix for Yorkshire pudding stood on the counter ready to hit the hot oven. The vegetables were simmering on the stove. How he loved his wife! Nary had a day passed that he didn't feel lucky to have her. She was so tidy and efficient in the kitchen; there was always a great dinner on the table, and she was always happy to greet him. Tonight was different. He could tell she wasn't happy, and he was about to find out why.

Jane entered the room, gave him a faint smile, then slipped into the booth across from him. They exchanged glances— his inquisitive, hers woeful. She gave him a wry smile. He detected a slight quiver on her chin.

"What gives?" Benjamin asked, swirling his drink like he was testing centrifugal force.

"It's Jonathan," she said. "Again."

"What is it this time?" The resignation in his voice was palpable.

She gave a sigh. "The police were here today."

"Police!" he exclaimed. "What could he possibly have done to warrant police action?"

A tear slid down her cheek like a dewdrop on a rose petal.

Benjamin reached for her hand as she blurted, "He vandalized the neighbour's car—that's what he's done!"

"You've got to be kidding! I don't believe it!"

"Just have a look out the window and you'll see for yourself."

Benjamin quickly disentangled his long legs from beneath the nook and strode across to the dining room window.

"I see a white Cadillac out there," he called across the room.

"Look at the windows and the wheels."

"Oh. Now I see what's been done. The windows are marked with something or other, and the air's out of the tires."

Precisely at that moment, Jonathan's music seemed louder, as if he could hear their conversation from the other side of the home. Jane stood beside Benjamin now and touched his arm.

"Are they pressing charges?" he queried.

"I don't know," Jane replied.

"How do they know it was Jonathan?" Ben's voice was husky. "It could have been anybody."

"You need to go over to the neighbours and speak to Mr. Halliday. Of course, Jonathan denies it."

"I'm going there right now." He turned to leave.

She grabbed his arm. "Please, Ben, can we have dinner first? The Yorkshire pudding is due to come out of the oven, and everything else is ready."

He stole a quick glance at the dining room table, all neatly set for three.

"Alright, I won't spoil dinner, nor will I talk to Jonathan about it until after I speak to Mr. Halliday."

***

Jonathan took his place at the table, thinking she must not have told his dad after all; he seemed normal. He was relieved she hadn't told him. He heaped potatoes on his plate, added asparagus and carrots, and barely found room for the tall Yorkshire pudding. Then he smothered everything with his mother's special gravy. He could never quite get enough of it. He always worked up an appetite when he played piano, but today after filling his plate he was so stressed, he couldn't taste any of it. He thought if he didn't eat, he'd appear guilty. Despite lack of appetite, he also managed to eat a small portion of chiffon cake before excusing himself from the table. As he walked away, unwelcome thoughts crowded his mind.

They hardly spoke to me tonight. She must have told him. She always tells him everything, even the little things. And this is a big thing, what with the police and all.

He'd planned to go to his room, look over his coin collection, and study his advanced mathematics textbook. Money and numbers always fascinated him. Instead, he took a detour and walked morosely back to his Steinway.

He looked up from his piano while his fingers once again found the notes of Bach. His glance out the window drew a chuckle when he saw the Halliday boys washing the crayon marks off the windows of their new Cadillac. But his chuckle soon faded into a gasp when he saw his dad on the street, speaking with their father. When they turned and walked into the Halliday house, Jonathan began to worry.

They can't know it was me. There was no one on the street when I snuck out of the house. There was no one. How can they blame me if they didn't see me?

"Son, we need to talk."

Jonathan's father returned from the Halliday's house fifteen minutes later. He'd pulled a chair up to the piano and straddled it. A cloud of seriousness covered his face. Jonathan squirmed on the piano bench before shifting around to face his father. His heart picked up a beat. He felt his mouth go dry.

"Why did you do it, Jonathan?" His voice was stern and his eyes bore right into his son.

"Do what, Dad?" He could hardly get the words out.

"You know very well what. You cannot wriggle out of it. I know you vandalized the neighbours' car. I just cannot, for the life of me, figure out why you would do such a thing."

"You can't prove I did it."

"Jonathan, I know you did it, so let's not go there. Let's not add lying to this dastardly deed. Look, if there's something bothering you, or you need something, or you feel deprived in some way, please tell me." His tone took on a softer tone. "Please tell me, son. I'm at a loss here to figure out why my son, who is from a good family, would stoop to such criminal action."

Jonathan sat quietly looking down, barely moving. He knew he was in for it, but still felt there was no proof. He decided silence was his best response as he waited for the punishment he knew was coming.

"Alright then, here's what's going to happen. It cost Mr. Halliday sixty dollars to have a truck come out and refill the tires. Sixty dollars is what you will to pay to Mr. Halliday."

"But you can't do that, Dad; I have some coins coming that I've been saving for."

"Well … you should have thought of that before you did it, Jonathan. Every action has a consequence. Haven't I told you that many times in the past? I want you to take sixty dollars from your savings and go over to their home tonight, apologize, and pay them for the expense you caused. If you don't, Mr. Halliday will press charges. Consider yourself lucky."

Jonathan swallowed hard and decided he would just get through it. Actually, it was all worth it for fixing that jerk next door with his smug face. He resigned himself to the punishment and swung around back to the keyboard.

"Turn around, we're not finished!" His father's voice was piercing. "And you will mow their lawn for the rest of the summer."

"What? Mow their lawn? Dad, you can't mean it! I can't do that, Dad." He could just see Brent and his brothers laughing at him when he was doing it.

Desperately trying to still the sobs that were building in his throat, Jonathan cried out, "Man, that really sucks! I can't do that! Why are you blaming me, anyway? I didn't touch their damn old car!"

"Be a man, son, and take responsibility for your actions. Someday you will thank me for this." Professor Brown turned his six-foot-four frame around and quickly crossed the room with long strides. If Jonathan had seen his father's face then, he would have seen the moisture in his eyes.

Jonathan stood for a few moments at the Halliday door, gaining the courage to ring the doorbell. He hoped Brent wouldn't answer the ring, and he didn't. Instead, Mr. Halliday opened the door like he was expecting him. He was a short man with kind eyes. Jonathan thrust his hand forward with the packet of money he'd been saving for his coins.

"I've been told to bring this over for the car. I didn't do it, but anyway here's the money that it cost you. And I've been told to apologize."

His sons began to giggle from behind their father, who quickly stepped out and shut the door behind him, closing off the sound. Jonathan's face turned red. This didn't go un-noticed by Mr. Halliday who, at that moment, must have realized there was something going on between the boys.

He accepted the money and thanked Jonathan for bringing it over. Before turning to go back into the house, he said, "I accept your apology."

Jonathan turned and started walking home, but something made him turn and look at the front door of the Halliday home. Then he saw it: a video camera mounted just above the front door, in direct line with the white Cadillac on the street. He was totally busted. He felt as though his face would fall off.

3

Exonerated

I was slammed back into my chair in front of the screen! Although the screen was blank now, in my mind's eye I could clearly see that camera strategically placed over the Halliday's door, capturing every movement of the devilry I'd so vehemently denied. Reliving that part of my life, it charged back at me. It showed the sadness I'd caused my parents, and it showed the kindness Mr. Halliday had shown me, despite all I'd done. Shame and regret reached into my very core, and for the very first time, I felt truly sorry.

Matthew turned to me and raised his brows as if to ask, "What do you have to say about that?" I noticed he had chocolate crumbs down the front of his apron. I glanced at the plate and saw it was empty.

I couldn't answer. My thoughts were mired in regret as I tried to add up all of the things I'd done in my youth and adult life, all of the things I'd done that I now realized were wrought through envy. There were too many to recall.

"Jonathan, I asked you a question. Please answer me."

"B-but I was just a kid," I stammered, using my last, small thread of defence.

His face softened and his smile told me he was conscious of my regret.

"Yes, you were just a kid, Jonathan, but I dare say at fourteen you should have known better. I used that particular example in your life to show how the rule for living on Earth—ENVY, especially when it amalgamates with jealousy, makes one execute terrible actions; that particular misdemeanour was trivial compared to others in your adult life."

He must know everything, absolutely everything, about my life.

The multitude of memories collided in my mind, each one vying for first place, each one more shameless than the other. It was as if he were looking into my very soul.

"I know you're frightened now, Jonathan, because of your envious past, but there's something you must understand; you'll not only be judged by your sins, you will also be judged by your good deeds. You will receive demerits for iniquities and merits for goodness, because we are all about fair play here, Jonathan. The captain of each station along your journey will select an important segment of your life, one that best illustrates how you handled a particular rule for living on Earth. How you measured up, so to speak. I can tell that choice of segment left you regretful. Do you have regrets? That's hypothetical. I shouldn't be asking you that, because I know you're very sorry. As I've stated, you will also be judged for your good deeds."

I studied him then, his withered face, silver hair, and shaking hand, but it was the deep light in his eyes that made me realize he possessed great sincerity and wisdom.

"B-Brent Halliday wasn't very n-nice to me," I stammered.

"He was also to blame for what happened."

"We cannot blame others for our actions. You alone are the master of that. You kept spying on him from across the fence, acting like the neighbourhood sleuth. You weren't minding your own business. Tell me what happened after you started mowing their lawn."

"I can't remember exactly, but I think things got better. It wasn't as bad as I thought it was going to be."

"No, it wasn't. I think your father was wise in his decision for your punishment. Allow me to refresh your memory. On the second week of your lawn mowing, the Hallidays' treasured little dog fell into the deep end of the pool while the family was having their dinner. When they heard the splash, they all came out of house just in time to see you turn off the lawn mower and dive in to save their dog. He showed the palm of his hand and raised his eyebrows as if to say, "You must remember that." He went on, "And when Brent was struggling with his math, you spent hours tutoring him. You even helped him get into college."

I recalled all of that and how Brent and I had become best buddies, but it was all the rest of my forty-two years that was holding me captive.

At this juncture, he picked up the empty plate and left the room, leaving me to stew on my own. He returned after what felt like an eternity, wheeling in a trolley with a scale so large, it barely fit on top. It had a basket on both sides;

the left was marked, *EVIL,* and the right was marked, *GOODNESS.* Stones the size of apples were piled on the second shelf of the trolley. He was short of breath and puffing by the time he had it wheeled in front of me.

After sizing up the situation, I braved to ask, "I beg your pardon, Matthew, but could you please tell me what all of this is for?" The visit back to Earth had taken the spunk right out of me.

"Well, Jonathan, I'm about to measure your life by weighing your demerits and merits to see if you can move on to the next station."

I noticed he mentioned demerits first. I immediately recalled some of them, and once again fear struck deep in my soul.

He reached into the pocket of his apron and extracted a sheaf of paper.

Is that my life? I wondered.

Matthew unfurled the paper and silently read what was scribed. He reached down, picked up a stone, and dropped it into the basket on the *EVIL* side. He kept reading and reaching for another stone and dropping one after the other on the *EVIL* side. The ugly clunk it made as it hit the basket grew louder with each stone. The basket was sinking down on the left and was close to touching the surface of the trolley.

I sucked in my breath, waiting for the sound of another stone.

He smiled at me teasingly as he held one up and slowly lowered it. This time he placed it in the basket marked GOODNESS; and this time a resounding, joyous *bing* filled the room. I heard several more *bings*, each progressively louder, each music to my ears. Now the scale was evenly balanced. There was one stone left. Which side would it be? What would happen if it landed in the EVIL side?

He waited, purposely testing my patience. After what seemed like an eternity, he raised his hand and suspended it, chuckling. Clearly, he was enjoying himself. The loud *bing* that it made brought me to my feet, clapping. I'd survived the sin of ENVY. Now I could move forward, but first I needed to ask him a very important question.

"Matthew, please tell me where I'm headed. I don't know where I'm going."

"Of course you don't know that, Jonathan, and it's only natural you should ask, but I'm surprised a smart man like you would not have figured it out by now." His voice was quivering.

"You're on your way to meet your Creator. Thus far, you have made it through the first station without punishment, and you're lucky; many are not. There are five stations in all. You have four left. I wish you luck."

"My Creator, my Creator," I whispered. "But I'm an atheist!"

"I know," he replied, giving me a wink and a grin.

Before I could say another word, I was propelled out the door and back onto the path.

4

Innards

*W*hat did Matthew mean when he said I was on my way to meet the Creator? That statement lay at the epicentre of my fear. *What's all this Creator business about?* Fearfully, I pondered my situation. Apparently I'd died and apparently my body, for all intents and purposes, was gone—all except my cognition and feelings. My mind was scrambling for answers. *Perhaps this is all a bad dream. Maybe I'll just awaken to my beautiful life and all will be the same as before: a great position with fabulous wages; a dutiful wife who never questions my whereabouts; bright, intellectual sons studying their way to prosperity; and my luscious mistress always there for me, always willing and ready to provide a soft place for me to land, never asking for anything more* *than my company once a week.* My life on Earth was perfect. Oh please, let this all be a dream!

I considered myself to be a highly intelligent man. How else could I have risen to the high position in finance that I enjoyed? So why couldn't I figure this out?

What I found most puzzling was the phantom body I now possessed, along with its gliding motion, and the nebulous attitude from the person of happenstance who called himself the Explainer.

Huh, he never explained a damn thing. He was such an arrogant man! He needed to be taken down a notch. I should have done it. I recalled exercising my talent for this at boardroom meetings when some upstart became too opinionated. Matthew, on the other hand, was much more accommodating. He at least explained where I was supposedly heading. And another thing... he didn't smirk.

I also wondered what comprised the other four Rules for Living on Earth, and why the Explainer or Matthew hadn't spelled them out to me. I realized now that I might not know until I arrived at each station, but there shouldn't be any harm, I rationalized, in pressing for an answer at the next station. On Earth we would call that being proactive. It seemed a rather silly statement now.

I also wondered if I were going to be catapulted back to Earth like I was for ENVY. The pangs of regret from that stop-over remained like a sack of hammers heavy on my chest.

I glanced to my left to see if the other phantoms were still following, and to my surprise they were gone. The scenery was changing and slowly coming to life, like the dawning of a new day. I saw a beautiful, sandy shore with blue waves lapping against it. On the distant land, I saw some straw huts with teepee-type tops. A warm sun was beaming from an azure-blue sky.

What land is this? I don't recognize it. Where can it be?

Next I saw an open field with animals here and there, and I had my answer. The grazing giraffes, their long necks arching to nibble leaves, and elephants tugging at the branches of trees gave me the answer.

AFRICA! It could be no other. I'm looking at Africa.

No sooner did this scene explain itself than it was changing again. This time, two sailing ships came into my line of vision. *Henrietta Maria* was painted on the bow of the first ship. It sat in deeper waters near a rock outjut. Several men were standing on the deck, taking turns looking through a telescope toward shore.

As I approached the shore, I saw a large, black man wearing a yellow robe and an elaborate, red-feathered headdress. He was leading several scantily-clad, young black men and women, apparently under duress, for he was wielding a switch should they step out of line. He met a white man at water's edge who stepped out from a flotilla of canoes. The white man handed him a small sack and they shook hands to seal some kind of bargain. With a great measure of resistance, the almost naked youths were forced into the canoes, leaving a group of other people I assumed were relatives wailing and crying and falling down on the shore. It didn't take me long to recognize this horrendous scene as the enforcement of chattel slavery I'd studied in my history class at school.

The scene advanced and I saw the other ship harboured nearby. It had *Jesus of Rubeck* written along its side. I glanced beyond at the vastness of the land, its wild, free animals, and golden grasses swaying in the breeze, interspersed by full trees with low, outstretched branches as though they were embracing this beautiful land. But soon this wondrous vista became contaminated, blemished beyond description, when I saw several Caucasian men dragging young black men and women, gagged so effectively they could only moan, and bound so tightly they could only hobble as they were forced toward the shore. A burly man walking alongside brandished a switch. I saw other white men approaching the shore with chains and ropes looped around their arms as they searched for more slaves. And again, many others were sorrowfully jumping up and down on the beach, screaming and crying. The lament was hard on my ears and harder still on my emotions. The sorrow I felt reached the pit of my heart as I watched these people being wrenched from their homeland.

The scene on the left faded away, and I was back to seeing phantom people on the same trek as myself. I decided to look to the right where, instead of more phantom people, a new scene from the past presented itself. Many black people were hunched over, picking cotton balls. The cotton field stretched over a large area like a big, white quilt. In the distance, a pillared, two-storey residence stood proudly against the skyline. The drone of call and response pattern of repetitious singing emanated from the cotton fields. I couldn't hear all of the phrases, but I did hear these words: "Oh Lordie, jump down, pick a bale of cotton, and bring the cotton down," being sung over and over again, interspersed by inaudible verses in a lamenting, sombre tune. Then that scene faded and another replaced it. A great march of many black people was happening, led by a man, clearly one of distinction considering how he had the power to create such a following. The song from the cotton fields had stopped and a clear voice declared in familiar words, "Free! Free at last! Thank God Almighty, we are free at last!"

Before I could wrap my mind around all of these scenes, a large convention hall appeared in the foreground, and I glided through the front door. I was astonished to see hundreds of phantoms like myself seated there. I was the last to enter and glided to a centre seat in the front row. The large stage in front of me was vacant, with the exception of a microphone and podium situated at centre front. I glanced up and around. The ceiling was high, with an enormous light fixture representative of a disco ball. The walls were painted in a soft blue and also had similar-type light fixtures evenly mounted every six feet around the room. Needless to say, the room was bright, cheerful, and arresting.

A tall, elegant lady dressed in a long, white, flowing gown with a royal-blue cape walked elegantly up to the podium. She smiled and greeted the audience.

"Good evening, everyone. My name is Elizabeth. I represent the Creator." She spoke in a soft, melodious voice through smiling lips, exposing beautiful, white teeth.

So, it's evening now, I thought. Funny, so far on this trek of mine, I hadn't considered what time of day it was. And despite the fully-packed auditorium, I felt as though she were speaking only to me.

"Welcome to station number two. I'm sure you all have guessed what Rule for Living on Earth will be discussed here. Would anyone care to tell us?"

My hand shot up like a jack-in-the-box—so fast, in fact, that I thought my arm had left its socket.

"Prejudice," I shouted, instantly embarrassing myself with my schoolboy exuberance. After all, one didn't have to be a rocket scientist to figure that one out.

I felt the warmth of her eyes as she looked me, as though I were special.

"That's absolutely correct, Jonathan. To be more exact, the rule is, Do Not Be Prejudiced."

She knows my name, just like the others did. I felt naked.

At this, an ominous, black sign fell onto the stage with a thud, making everyone in the room jump in their chairs. It landed below the podium. The words in bright red, *do not be prejudiced*, wound across its surface like a snake. They, whoever they were, certainly had special effects down pat.

The gentle lady continued, "You all have witnessed, at the birth of America, how sad the slave trade was, and you all have witnessed the prejudice against the colour of another's skin. And you all have learned about the Civil War in school and when slavery was abolished. Today I have shown you the determination of the marchers to be equal in every way.

"What we will discuss today at this forum is the many different kinds of prejudice practiced on Earth, how each and every one of you took part and practiced prejudice, and how each of you has been affected by it. I can hear many of you thinking that you were never prejudiced. There are very few, if any, people on Earth who have not practiced or been affected by prejudice in one form or another. Let's establish some of them. Could someone from the back row give me another form of prejudice practiced on Earth?"

A voice boomed from the back, "The Holocaust and prejudice against the Jewish people; that was the worst of all! Why didn't you demonstrate that?"

"Yes, Evan, I wanted the Holocaust spoken aloud, so I left it for you to bring up, as I knew you would … and rightly so. The Holocaust, with all of the sorrow, pain, and suffering brought to the Jewish people, was a scourge on mankind with lasting effects. Your family and many others suffered beyond measure. The Jewish people have suffered for centuries in many ways. Prejudice against nationalities and religion remains on Earth today and is the cause of most wars."

"What about prejudice against gay men?" a man shouted.

"And lesbians?" echoed a lady's voice.

"And the fat and the thin?" was offered from the middle of the room.

"Ah yes," Elizabeth said. "Mankind early on established what was considered to be normal, and anyone outside that parameter has been ostracized. It has taken centuries for some, but unfortunately not all, to realize normal has many dimensions. Consequently, many who are what they were born to be have suffered." Her voice was soft and soothing.

A sigh could be heard rippling throughout the room.

I sat pondering my life I wanted to shout aloud that I had never been prejudiced. As a matter of fact, I was becoming increasingly annoyed with the whole subject. But I was forced to listen.

It was as though she was reading my mind when she asked, "Can you give me examples of other kinds of prejudice?" She extended her palms across the auditorium, raising them up and down.

"Prejudice against ugly people and the crippled ones," squeaked a woman sitting in a wheelchair directly behind me.

"Yes, that's correct, Sky. Not only did you struggle with your affliction, but you also had to deal with prejudice because of it."

I could hear the sorrow in her voice.

"Prejudice against the poor and underprivileged," shouted someone from the far-right corner of the room.

"Again," said Elizabeth, "the poor and underprivileged and also the aged pay a penalty twice-fold. Mankind has been so cruel. Gratefully, there are those who try to help, but percentage-wise, they are few. Life on Earth has shown that some educated people look down on the folks who aren't as educated, and they feel it's beneath them to associate with underlings. That too is sad. You see, everyone is created equal. All people on Earth have been created equal.

"I want you all to repeat after me: all people are created equal."

The audience shouted so loudly it hurt my ears. *For Pete's sake, she's treating us like school children.* I didn't follow suit; the whole thing was ridiculous. I'd listened to her soft voice expounding on prejudice ad nauseam. Again I pondered what was being said and felt totally innocent of any of it. Besides, I had a right to my opinions, which I shared with other successful men. We'd questioned the actuality of the Holocaust, rationalizing how many, many people had suffered during World War II.

I also felt justified in hiring only the *crème de la crème* of straight, white applicants for our many corporations. Why shouldn't I have the right to do that? After all, it was my hard-earned money financing these enterprises. And why shouldn't I associate with only those of my class, of my intellect? Hadn't I spent years studying at university, and didn't I work hard for what I'd achieved in life? And now, damn it, I didn't know where I was, or where I was headed.

She must have noticed I was disgruntled; her eyes swung in my direction. I stood up and tried to will myself out of the hall, but my feet glided up to the stage in front of her as though she'd summoned me.

As I stood before her, I was astounded by her incredible beauty: sky-blue eyes with sweeping, black lashes, an oval face of dark but not black skin, indicative of a mixed race, and black hair that cascaded soft curls around her shoulders like an ebony shawl.

She smiled and said, "Yes, Jonathan?"

My voice was loud and crisp.

"When I arrived at the first stop, I was told by a man who called himself the Explainer—and who, by the way, didn't explain a damn thing—that I would have to pass the Rules for Living on Earth, but he refrained from telling me what these rules are. I know about Envy and now Prejudice. Needless to say, I'm curious about the rest. I was also told I'm headed to meet the Creator. Creator of what? The whole thing doesn't make any sense to me at all. It's preposterous and most unfair!"

"You have to be patient, Jonathan. You'll find out in good time."

"Patient?" I shouted, as anger washed over me. "You've taken my body and given me this ridiculous phantom thing in its place, moved me at a snail's pace up some kind of trail, then left me high and dry wondering about it all. And now you have the audacity to tell me to be patient. I think you and your so-called colleagues need a lesson in leadership."

She simply smiled and repeated in that sugary voice of hers, "I repeat, you must be patient, Jonathan. Just be thankful you aren't headed in the opposite direction." She released a low, throaty chuckle that was mimicked by others in the audience, causing a reverberation around the room. It roared in my ears, becoming louder by the second. My frustration was so strong, I felt as though I was about to hyperventilate. When she spoke again, the laughter ceased.

"We've covered the many different categories of prejudice and its ramifications. I don't think we've missed any."

A sudden breeze was blowing, making her blue cape look like angel wings. She took a whistle from the pocket of her flowing gown and blew it three times like a signal. And a signal it was, for a gentleman dressed in white pushed a trolley out onto the stage right in front of me.

In contrast to the trolley at Matthew's Envy station, it was pure white with a plastic cover over the top, obviously to conceal what was on top. The gentleman whipped off the cover with a swoop, exposing what was on the surface.

Good grief! I stood there with my mouth gaping.

There, spread before me, in various shades of what I could only describe as raw meat, I saw human innards placed strategically in five repetitive rows. I felt queasy.

As I stared at the innards, a screen dropped down behind the trolley with a thud, making me jump. Now the objects were projected upon it for all to see. I heard a gasp echo throughout the audience. Apparently, they were as shocked as I.

Elizabeth spoke with clarity. "Some of you will recognize what lies before us, others may not." She walked over and stood beside me. She pointed at each organ as she spoke.

"These are the vital organs of a human's inner works. We have the body's all-important pump, the heart; next, the lungs, which provide life's oxygen to the body. Then we have the stomach, which I call the fuel tank, and we have the kidneys that dispose of bodily fluid and toxins. And, of course, we have the brain, sitting on the throne at the top, directing all.

"Every person on Earth has been given exactly the same innards. All are generic; there are no special models. Jonathan, I want you to look at them carefully and tell the audience if you see a superior row. Tell them if you see any one row as being better than the other, any varia-tions between them."

I was dumbfounded to be given this ri-diculous task. It was hypothetical. She bloody well knew the answer. I hesitated with my response.

"I see you're hesitating. Would you like a magnifying glass, or perhaps a measuring tape?"

This brought a ripple of laughter through the audience, and I felt like a fool.

"No," I replied. "They all look exactly the same."

"Are you absolutely sure about that?" asked Elizabeth. She looked at me with piercing eyes. "I want you to study the last column on the right. Does it look superior in any way, Jonathan?"

I was totally frustrated by this time, and my reply came out more as a retort.

"No, it doesn't. I just told you all of them look exactly the same."

Her words that followed left me astounded.

"The organs on the right belong to you, Jonathan." She spoke in such a matter-of-fact way, with a nod of the head that annoyed me.

"Mine?" I exclaimed. It seemed clear to me they, whoever they were, were using shock value to get to me. "Did … did you take them out of my body at the accident site?"

She didn't answer my question.

"So you see, Jonathan, you're not superior to any other man on Earth. No better, no less, but equal. Now I want you to look into the audience."

With the appalling knowledge that my innards were lying on the trolley, I turned to the audience and was further astounded. Half were black, many wore skull caps or beanies, more correctly called the *yarmulke* to signify their Jewish custom. Others were same-sex couples holding hands, and the balance were Hispanics, East Indians, and First Nations, to name a few. And they were all smiling at me, almost sneering.

I was dumbstruck and couldn't think of anything to say. How could I look into the eyes of all of these smiling people and tell them I was superior?

"Do you see anyone out there to whom you are superior?" Her voice floated around me like sugar crystals.

Elizabeth waited for a few seconds, quietly tapping her fingers on the podium before speaking.

"I repeat, do you see anyone to whom you are superior?"

I stole a side glance at her, still in awe of her beauty, but didn't answer. Instead, I pointedly asked her a question.

"Are you accusing me of being prejudice?"

"I heard your thoughts, Jonathan, and I know you're in denial. On one hand, you tell yourself you're not prejudiced, and on the other, you defend the fact that because you worked hard, you have the right to be. Tell that to the black man in the audience to whom, despite his qualifications, you denied employment solely because of the colour of his skin. And tell the Jewish man that you have questioned the actuality of the Holocaust. Tell that to the long-suffering Jewish people in the audience who watched their entire families being annihilated. Clearly you *have* been prejudiced and have broken that rule for living on Earth."

She held my gaze for a several moments while her words found their mark. I broke the spell and looked out to the audience, taking notice again of all of the black, Jewish, and ethnic people. They were shaking their heads from side to side, *tsking* and clucking their tongues in disgust. Before I could react emotionally to this taunting, the entire audience followed suit, with the exception of an elderly Jewish man and a middle-aged black man who sat stoically in the front row.

I, who was far more accustomed to applause, was now having to endure this horrible cacophony of sound, which was growing louder and louder, jabbing at my every nerve while rubbing away my old feelings of prejudice. I stood there like an idiot feeling so ashamed of what those feelings were. Finally, much to my chagrin, I was crying uncontrollably. Tears flowed down my cheeks and neck and onto my phantom shirt, making it feel wet and itchy against my chest. I was truly sorry. I felt like a rag that had been dragged through a waterhole.

Elizabeth raised her arms with palms up and silenced the room, leaving only the last of my ebbing sobs. She spoke in a velvet voice.

"Jonathan, I know you're sorry for breaking the Rule of Prejudice, but remember we also have to look at your good deeds in this time of your life, so please keep a stout heart."

No matter how hard I tried, I couldn't recall anything I'd done to offset my failure. That, along with the jeering, left me feeling totally doomed. Then to my surprise, the Jewish man sitting in the front row, who hadn't jeered, jumped to his feet.

"Wait a minute!" he shouted. "I have something to say." He spoke with a marked Jewish-New York accent.

"Irving Goldberg, please take it easy. I know what's on your mind. We need to have Jonathan back in his seat before we hear you."

The return to my seat was so instant, I didn't know what had happened first—her words or my return.

"Ladies and gentlemen, Mr. Goldberg has a story to tell us about Jonathan. As he's relating this story, I will project his thoughts and words onto the screen in the form of a short movie for you all to see."

At this juncture, two men came onto the stage and removed the trolley with its gruesome contents. Simultaneously, the screen increased in size and the room darkened. There was a hush throughout the auditorium that only moments earlier had been filled with heckling. Now as everyone settled back to watch the movie, again as strange as it was earlier, I could smell lilacs and lemons as the story unfolded.

As the aerial view of New York City came to life on the screen, the front entrance of the Sinai Hospital was zeroed in on, showing the doors opened wide with all of its hustle and bustle inside: doctors being paged, staff walking the long corridors with charts in hand, and cleaning staff on their assignments while the whining of an ambulance burped to a stop outside the emergency room. Simultaneously, a soft male voice began the narration:

"Most widows have to struggle, but no one more than Rachel Esselstein since the untimely death of her husband three years ago. She has had to work at many different types of employment, sometimes two jobs at the same time, just to support herself and her ten-year-old son, Liam. Things were much different when Jeremiah was alive. The small general store they operated in New Westminster, British Columbia, near the Fraser River, gave them a comfortable existence, but after Jeremiah's death in 2008, inflation struck and Rachel was forced to sell. She took on several different office jobs during the day, and in the evenings she cleaned office buildings.

"She was grateful to the kind neighbour who was looking after Liam. Liam, the son Jeremiah had longed for, had been left without a father. Remembering the clinical smell of the hospital, Rachel recalled daily her husband's words from his bedside. Let's look back on them now when Liam was here in this hospital and listen to their hospital conversation."

"Oy vey, I don't think I'll live to be at Liam's Bar Mitzvah. Who will take my place? Who will teach my son to read from the Torah? Who will instill in him how to be a man—a good Jewish man? I'm so sad for my Liam!"

Rachel swallowed hard but couldn't rid herself of the lump in her throat. She looked at her husband's wasted body as he lay in bed, then reached over and smoothed the last of his hair.

"Oh darling, Liam will be just fine. And don't you be talking that way. Dr. Meshnik says you have a good chance with the chemo. And besides, your brother, Abe, will be our mentsh. He'll pitch in and help. He'll be visiting you this afternoon."

"Promise me, Rachel. Liam should have a good Bar Mitzvah. You know our special account is there for any expense. I've been saving for this a long time. I must get Abe to promise to help."

With eyes brimming over, he reached for the blanket and pulled it up to his chin. Rachel could see the artery throbbing in his wrist.

"And now I won't be there to witness!"

He covered both cheeks with his hands.

"Those words spoken three years earlier were very fresh in Rachel's mind—syllable by syllable, word for word—fresher still now that Liam was quickly approaching his thirteenth year. Nary a day passed that she didn't recall them, hearing again the sad tone of her husband's voice as she relived his pain. Her sorrow, though constant, had dimmed in its intensity.

"Liam, despite the loss of his father, was developing nicely into a young man. His voice had changed and he was growing strong. His Uncle Abe had stepped right up to the plate as a surrogate father, offering support, arranging outings for Liam, and picking him up for weekend stays at his home at the other end of town. In preparation for his Bar Mitzvah, he taught him to read from the Torah and chant in Hebrew.

"And Rachel was busy too, baking for the celebration party and planning the big dinner all of the other relatives and friends would attend. Every spare moment she had she spent baking, planning, and talking it over with her friends to ensure it would be an unforgettable celebration for Liam when he marked his entry into manhood, just as his father had dreamed and spoken of so frequently before his death.

"And while the home was permeating with the smell of vanilla and cinnamon and freshly baked bread, the word *Bar Mitzvah* was rolling off Rachel's tongue almost every moment of the day. *God should give my Liam health and happiness.*

"The celebration would begin by going to Temple, with Liam reading from the Torah and chanting in Hebrew, just as his uncle Abe had trained him to do. Afterwards in the hall, they would have a luncheon of traditional Jewish foods, all kosher and appropriate, and they would eat the *challah*, the braided Jewish bread she'd spent hours baking.

"The next day there would be a wonderful sit-down, beef dinner for friends and relatives where Liam, dressed in his new navy suit, white shirt and tie, and wearing his *yarmulke,* would stand before the microphone and give his first speech, all under the guidance of his surrogate father, Uncle Abe, who'd taken on his task with unbelievable exuberance and dedication, making it difficult to tell who was more excited about this great event—Liam or his uncle.

"But there were to be big, black clouds in the sky for Abe.

Three days before Liam's eventful weekend, Abe and the other auditing personnel at the Royal Bank were summoned to the boardroom. The note on his desk late the prior day had an ominous ring. It read: CRITICAL MEETING SLATED IN THE BOARDROOM FOR 10:00 A.M. SHARP! It was signed with the branch manager's indisputable signature. The next morning, six men with auditing credentials entered the boardroom. One by one they entered, all of them wondering why they'd been summoned.

"Tall, floor-to-ceiling, plate glass windows on the sixteenth floor in the west end of New York City could not prevent the brilliant sunshine from flooding the room, nor inhibit the view of many other buildings all around, with like-windows creating a menagerie of sun-kissed shining glass. The oak table in the middle of the room, gleaming like a new penny, was surrounded by stuffed, straight-back chairs in a deep maroon colour. The table could easily seat a dozen, but only one end was to be occupied today. The pungent aroma of coffee and the sound of it gurgling and dripping into the carafe at the side credenza was an invitation to partake.

"Abe Esselstein was last in line to fill his mug. It was too late for him to be selective about where to sit; consequently, he found himself beside his colleague, Donald, who always wore too much cologne. It was also too late to move to the other side without insulting him.

"*Why does Donald always plaster himself with that stuff? Someone should tell the klutz,* Abe thought.

"Those thoughts did not linger long before Liam's Bar Mitzvah took over; in fact, it was all he'd been able to think about for many weeks now."

At the front of the room stood an easel affixed with a large map of South America. There were three coloured pins designating two cities in Brazil and one off the coast in Belize.

The other men sat in quiet chatter at the table, sipping their coffee, but the ominous summons hung in the room like a fog, marking their faces with anxiety. Little wonder a hush descended upon the room and all heads swung quickly to the door when the knob was turned.

"Good morning, gentlemen," the bank manager's voice boomed. "I see you have helped yourselves to the coffee." Loose change in his pocket jingled as he walked with heavy feet up to the front of the room. He placed his attaché case on a desk with a thud and snapped it open. He took out a sheaf of papers, laid them on the podium near the easel, and cleared his throat.

"Gentlemen, thank you for coming on such short notice. Let's get right down to business, shall we? As you can see on the map, the addresses of three branches of our investment firm have been pinpointed—two in Brazil, and one in Belize. We've received word from a secret informant that a classic case of embezzlement is and has been in progress for several months. Needless to say, this is causing a crisis, the worst I've seen in all my twenty-five years with the bank. Our president and chief executive officer is flying in from Vancouver, Canada for a first visit. He is expected momentarily."

A tall, strikingly handsome, dark-haired man filled the doorway. Distinguished in his black, silk suit, he took long, confident strides toward the manager and shook his hand. They conversed in a whisper for a few moments, then turned toward the auditors.

The manager announced, "Gentlemen, I'd like to introduce the president of our bank, Mr. Jonathan Brown."

Abe, jarred back from his thoughts of the Bar Mitzvah, glanced around the room at anxious-faced colleagues. Abe was anxious too—anxious to get this over with and head back to his office to get on with other things. Nonetheless, his curiosity was peaked.

Jonathan Brown cleared his throat and spoke in a deep, baritone voice, reiterating what the manager had said.

"Gentlemen, a very serious situation has recently come to light that is in need of our investigation." He gestured toward the map. 'In the three cities indicated here, a classic case of money laundering and embezzlement is possibly in progress. We need to get to the bottom of it … Immediately!" He paused momentarily, allowing his words to register, then cleared this throat and continued speaking in a louder voice. "We need two men to audit and track the accounts. We need a man to be disguised as an employee at each branch, but more importantly, we need a capable man to coordinate, plan, and oversee the entire operation!"

Jonathan studied the anxious faces before him: studious, well-groomed, typical financial lot waiting to be challenged with a number crunching assignment. He recalled being at the opposite end of the spectrum, when as a young bank manager, the auditors would come in and take over the accounts like they owned the place. He'd never held them in high esteem until today—today he really needed them. Bright sunlight streaming through the glass-enclosed room made them squint. He must tell the manager here to install suitable draperies if he wanted his boardroom to be more effective, he thought.

His audience looked around at each other, wondering where they would fit in. What part of the investigation would management assign to them? Abe's heart quickened as he thought about next week's Bar Mitzvah.

Jonathan spoke again with brows knit and eyes piercing.

"I realize I've given you very brief overview, but I'll be happy to answer any questions you might have as best I can. Yes?" He pointed to a man who had his hand up.

"How did you learn of the problem?"

"From an insider, that's all I can tell you."

"How much money is missing?" asked another.

"We're not sure of numbers yet. We're also not absolutely sure about the em-bezzlement. We haven't ruled out employee error yet, but we're not taking any chances. This kind of thing can really gallop if not caught early."

He raised his index finger for emphasis. "I'd rather find out one way or the other as soon as possible by covering all bases and going in on the sole premise of embezzlement." He couldn't have spoken more emphatically.

"How soon do we get started?" asked Abe, hoping it would be after the Bar Mitzvah.

"Yesterday," replied Jonathan without hesitation. "Yesterday. That's the urgency of it. My private plane is waiting on the tarmac at the airport as we speak. We fly out early tomorrow morning. You will do your packing this evening."

Abe felt like he was being squeezed between the jaws of a vice. He couldn't possibly miss his nephew's big day and break his promise to his dead brother, but when promoted to this auditing position, he'd pledged never to refuse an assignment. That day he felt like he'd risen in the helium balloon of success. And now …

Jonathan continued, "You will now go back to your offices, and in a few moments you'll be given your auditing location and assignment. I would ask, however, that Abe Esselstein please remain behind."

The gentlemen stood up like robots, placed their cups on the sideboard, and one by one left the boardroom. They glanced inquisitively at Abe as they walked by, clearly wondering why he'd been asked to remain behind.

Abe sat transfixed. The taste of coffee lingered in his mouth as he sat staring at a patch of light on the table. He knew they would ask him to head the assignment. But how could he possibly let Liam down now, after all of their rehearsing and studying? Liam, who had become the son he never had. He could not disappoint him. He could not break the promise he'd made to his dying brother. It was locked in his heart, and he could never break it. He must attend Liam's Bar Mitzvah without question.

The manager and Jonathan took a seat across from him at the table. Jonathan spoke first.

"Abe, after much deliberation, we've decided you should be the man to head this project. I've looked at your record, and it stands for itself. You have an analytical mind, a fierce dedication, and you also have one of the highest records of success in your profession. We need you in charge."

Stymied, Abe drew in his breath as he tried to unscramble his thoughts. In the past when he was stuck, he always reverted to his upbringing. Honesty was the best policy. It had always helped him out in the past. Yes, the best approach was honesty.

"I thank you for putting such faith in me, but I have a huge problem."

"A problem?" retorted the bank manager, who was flushing right up to his hairline. "You have a problem? It's not you that has a problem … it's your employer that has the problem. We're facing a possible embezzlement worth hundreds of thousands of dollars. You will leave on the first plane tomorrow." His mouth clamped to a fine line and his jaw tightened.

"I cannot go," replied Abe. "I'm sorry. I cannot go … I-I have to"

"You have to what?" barked the bank manager.

"Just a minute," said Jonathan. He turned to the bank manager. "Let's hear him out. What's your problem, Abe?"

"You see, it's like this," Abe spoke slowly, with deliberation. "Three years ago, my only brother died. As he lay on his death bed, I promised to take care of his son, Liam—to help him grow up to be a good Jewish man, to take charge of his Bar Mitzvah, to make sure his celebration into manhood is conducted in the best pos-sible way. His father saved money for this celebration, saved since the day Liam was born. The Bar Mitzvah is scheduled for next week."

Abe's mouth was suddenly dry and he reached for his coffee cup, but it was empty.

"Go on," said Jonathan.

"Well, we've been practising for days now. We practised how to chant and how to read from the Torah and how to give a short speech. And I've been talking with his mother on the organization of all the events. I will be escorting Liam and acting like his surrogate father. I cannot let him down now. I just can't. I know how important this mission is too. Oy vey, I just don't know what to do."

The bank manager sat drumming his fingers on the table in frustration. The silence in the room was palpable, with Abe's words hanging in the air. Finally, Jonathan spoke.

"I want to commend you on your loyalty to your nephew, Abe, and all you have done for him. I know how important a Bar Mitzvah is to a young Jewish boy. You must not miss it. I'll find someone to replace you. And I don't want you to worry about it.' He turned to the bank manager, adding, "It's the right thing to do."

The bank manager gave a small gasp. Abe could see surprise that bordered on anger in his face. Jonathan must have seen it also, for he turned to him and said, "There will be no repercussions."

Abe's sigh took with it all of his angst and tension as relief flooded over him. He stood up and walked around the table and exuberantly shook Jonathan's hand, then walked out the door with the sun shining on the little bald patch at the back of his head.

The bank manager turned to Jonathan. "My auditors made a pledge when they took office that they would always be available. Now I believe that all goes down the drain. A new precedent has been set. The apple cart of availability has just been turned over. Damn it all!"

"Why don't you contact Abe immediately and insist upon discretion? He looks like a man you can trust."

The bank manager walked over to the side table and picked up the phone. He appeared to be in a better mood when he returned, but there was still a little ice in his voice. "What are you going to do now?"

"Well, to be honest, your Abe was not my first choice. I know a gentleman from South Carolina, a black man who equals, if not surpasses, Abe's investigative talents. I know he's available."

Jonathan reached inside his lapel for his cell phone.

A roar of applause filled the auditorium as the lights came on. Abe and the black man, who had been seated next to me in the front row, sprang to their feet and began pumping my hand. I saw gratitude in their eyes but sat trying to make sense of the whole thing. I'd forgotten all about the kindness I'd shown the Jewish man, and how I'd given a black man the very important auditing assignment—an assignment that could very well have given me tremendous financial grief. I came to the realization that my life was a contradiction. My thoughts and mindset contradicted my actions—so much, in fact, that a moment ago I couldn't remember any of my good deeds, but now I enveloped all.

Then the thought occurred to me that both of these men must have also died, else I wouldn't be seeing them. I was truly sorry for the prejudice I'd harboured on Earth, and I felt a profound sense of gratitude for the kindness I'd shown both of them. Oh, how I hoped it was enough to move me forward to the next station.

It was.

I was propelled out the door and sent on my way with the jubilant applause of the audience ringing in my ears. My prejudices had been wiped away like drawing a brush across a blackboard.

5

Robin

Once again the path was before me and I was on my way. And once again I felt the frustration of not knowing where I was headed. After passing through the rules of envy and prejudice, I wondered what I would face next.

There appeared to be something different this time. I was being propelled a little more swiftly than before, and a certain kind of peace swept over me. Then I saw a robin flying ahead of me. He would land and wait for me, then as though guiding me, he would fly ahead with his red breast shining under the brilliant sunlight. His direction took me into a new territory where the path was replaced by soft green grass flanked by a multitude of flowers of every description and colour;

their beauty and wonderful scent fairly took my breath away.

There was so much coming at me all at once. Ahead a grove of trees sprung up— every species imaginable, from dark coniferous to white birch with fluttering leaves. Over the treetops across the sky to the west, a dark cloud appeared. I could hear a roll of thunder followed by a cloud burst. It was short-lived, for right on its heels was a vivid rainbow, the brightest I'd ever laid my eyes upon. Off in the distance to the right I could see a sky full of birds and a great field of animals of every description. Next to it, the blue of the ocean caught my eye. There was a variety of fish leaping from its surface.

How beautiful nature is, I thought. I couldn't remember appreciating it as much as I did at this moment. Although I was mesmerized by the vista before me, I couldn't help asking this question: "What is the purpose of all of this? Am I being primed for what is to come?"

Suddenly, the robin soared away high up into the sky. Simultaneously, a man's voice said, "Hello there, come and join me."

I was stopped and I turned my head to see a smiling man seated on a rock. He gestured to me to be seated on a boulder beside him. I was moved there. The air was filled with the scent of roses.

"Hello, Jonathan, my name is David. Welcome to station number 3. This is your third rule for living on Earth. The rule is called: Take Care of Mother Earth, Your Gift from the Creator.

The Creator. The word stuck in my throat. *So that's why all of these beautiful things came to the fore—the flowers, the birds, the animals, the trees, and the rainbow, all of the things from Earth advertising the Creator. I'm an atheist; all of these things came from a pure hydrogen, nebula cloud followed by the big bang, so to speak. I'd rather believe that than the Adam, Eve, and snake parable. This Creator business is just a bunch of bunk.* I held fast to my thought.

I tried shifting back a bit on the rock to get a better look at this man seated beside me, this man called David. But I was only afforded a glimpse of his profile and curly, blond hair until he turned toward me and I saw his face. He was young, at least a decade younger than I. His eyes were sky-blue. The happy countenance he sported told me he was ready to smile in a second's notice.

Speaking in a soft tone, he asked, "Did you take care of the Earth when you lived there?"

Before I could answer, he continued, "That was a hypothetical question. I already know the answer. You championed the cause. You put yourself forward on every turn."

I was baffled. *What on Earth is he talking about?*

"I'm puzzled," I replied. "Are you complimenting me on something I did? It will be a first for this particular road trip and a good thing too, because I don't think I have any more regrets left in me. Please enlighten me, David."

The smile that had been waiting to burst forward came full force, displaying glowing white teeth. He threw his head back and laughed.

"Well now, enlightening you, as you put it, will be my pleasure. It will be delivered to you in two parts. First, for part one, I thought it might be interesting to read you a short story about your life on Earth and how you did your part. I like hearing myself read and I think I'm pretty good at inflecting and using expression." To accentuate his boast, he blew on his finger tips and tapped his right shoulder.

Smiling, he reached down on the grass and picked up a book, scattering several butterflies—large monarchs and delicate, powder-blue summer azures. I could hear a crow cawing in the background while a snail on the ground stuck its head out from under its shell and pointed its antennae in that direction as if to the sound. A light breeze blew between the trees, rustling leaves. There was an earthy smell in the air.

"Well, let's get comfortable then, shall we?"

He opened the book, found the first page, and bent the book backward to straighten and give some flex to the spine. The noise of the birds, animals, and wind had suddenly stopped. All was silent as David's voice filled the air. His voice was musical, almost as if he were singing.

"Jonathan Brown walked up the sidewalk of the Regional District with the brochure on waste management in hand. He was attending the first meeting of the city and surrounding area on the all-important subject of waste disposal. It was especially important tonight, as it was hoped plans would be formed to deal with all of the waste in the city. He wouldn't have missed it for the world. When he arrived in the large auditorium, two engineers from the provincial government were up at the front of the room. There was a capacity crowd with more coming in. The attendants were scrambling for chairs.

"Jonathan said, 'Excuse me, excuse me,' as he slid in front of people to an empty chair in the middle of the row near the front. The large screen in place indicated there was going to be a slideshow. He was anxious to see it.

"'Can I have your attention, please? My name is Ed Jackson. I'm with the Waste Management Branch of British Columbia. I'm here tonight to present a slideshow on how the garbage and refuse of this city, which has grown exponentially over the years, has impacted our lives. Lights, please.'

"The lights were dimmed and the slide show began. The audience gasped when shown mountains of refuse piled high in an area as far as the eye could see. A lone backhoe was pushing the pile higher while a stream of garbage trucks dumped more, giving little hope of accomplishment to the operator. Squawking birds of all description were flying overhead, vying for bits of food.

"'As you can see, ladies and gentlemen, we are being overrun by our own garbage. What you cannot see are the greenhouse gases rising like a cloud from the pile and evaporating into the air. This is upsetting the balance of nature and contributing to global warming.'

"He stopped the slide, leaving the picture of the refuse on the screen.

"'As of January 1, we will be initiating a new method of getting rid of the garbage. This is what we're proposing. Each resident will separate their garbage into three piles: recyclables, which will include plastics and food containers; paper products, such as newspapers and magazines; and the third will be the food wastes—left over food items, and other items. You will be given a list for all three.'"

"A gentleman stood up in the third row and shouted, 'What? Do you mean to tell me I have to sort my garbage? What the hell am I paying taxes for?'

"Another man at the far end of the room echoed the first, adding, 'I'm not going to pay my taxes, and I'll get all my friends to stop as well. As a matter of fact, I'll get the whole damn street to stop paying taxes; then you'll change this cockamamie idea!'

"Several 'yeahs' could be heard around the room."

At this juncture, David looked up from the book and gave me a broad wink. I understood why when he continued to read:

"The noise level in the room soared as the crowd became engrossed in loud conversation. Jonathan Brown sprang to his feet and shouted above the din, 'What's the matter with you numbskulls?'

"He sidestepped across the front of people in his row, anxious to get to the front. One lady whispered to the other, 'I think I've seen that man at the bank.' When Jonathan reached the front, he took the microphone from the engineer and drew in a deep breath to settle his exasperation. His voice thundered across the auditorium.

"'Ladies and gentlemen, it is incumbent upon us all to protect our environment. The truth of the matter is, this is the twentieth century, and garbage needs to be sorted. How many here want an increase in taxes? If we expect the city to do it, they'll have to hire many new employees. That will undoubtedly make our taxes soar. I say that we all have to do our share.' He'd wanted to say, 'Do you expect the city to flush your toilets for you?' But he'd thought better of it.

"Murmuring filled the room. A few pivotal seconds passed before applause of gratitude broke out. The engineer thanked Jonathan for his intervention and continued with his presentation. Small pamphlets describing the recycling were passed out amongst the receptive crowd."

David closed the book, smiled, and said, "Who knows where things might have gone if you hadn't taken a stand. Planet Earth surely thanks you for that."

"That was nothing. I barely remember the evening," I replied, a mite bewildered.

I recalled with a mixture of fear and joy the previous stations of Envy and Prejudice I'd passed through, and how I'd been shown the error of my ways, but so far at this station, surrounded by the beauty of nature, I was being complimented.

"I know you're puzzled by the accolade we give you. We play fair on this, your infamous journey, commending when it's deserved, but we'll shake the core of your repentance when you have failed."

He turned the book around to show me the cover, which displayed two robins holding a banner with their beaks. Printed in the centre of the banner was the name, "Jonathan."

Puzzled, I wondered how they knew me and why they'd put so much emphasis on a logical response in a public forum.

As if he was reading my mind, David continued, "What I read just now pales by comparison with another stand you took, earlier on—one that reached deep into your pocket."

I scratched my brain but for the life of me I couldn't think of another thing I'd done for the Earth. Sure, I'd given household waste and leaves back to the Earth by composting, but that was nothing—nothing that the whole neighbourhood wasn't doing. What made me so special?

"I cannot for the life of me recall anything else I may or may not have done to protect the Earth," I admitted.

"I see," said David. "Come with me and I'll show you. I need to take you somewhere."

I glided behind him as he walked down a woodland path. The smell of the forest filled my nostrils, and my senses stirred at the sheer beauty all around me—wildflowers, mushrooms, ferns, and patches of lime-green moss dotting the forest floor. Tall coniferous trees spread their branches wide as though protecting it all. I felt the soft breeze against my cheek as it rustled the leaves in the grove of white birches. I strained my ears as I tried to identify the song birds that were filling the air with their melodious sound.

We came to a vacant patch in the forest where two hammocks were strung between trees. David pointed at one and said, "I want you to lie down there. I'll rest on

the other. I want you to close your eyes.
When you do, you will be transported back
to Earth, where you will relive that past
section of your life and will be judged
on how you protected the planet Earth and
its delicate ecosystem."

Now I had to face myself again. At least
this time it would be for the good, yet I
felt apprehensive.

David moved to the other hammock and
lay on it, saying, "This is so comfortable, I could stay here all day." He must
have sensed my apprehension and was trying to encourage me. He began whistling
a slow song as his hammock swayed back
and forth.

I sat down on the other hammock, dan-
gling my phantom feet. I watched the light
breeze zigzagging a leaf to the ground. It
seemed to parallel my feelings: sometimes
moving on my volition and other times not;
always filled with apprehension, not knowing what station I would come to and who I
would meet next. I'd successfully passed
though the ports of Envy and Prejudice,
but now I was being returned to my earth-
ly life to be judged further on how I
took care of planet Earth. Obviously, my
stand at the Regional District meeting
didn't suffice.

I lay back on the hammock and gazed upwards. The northern lights in all their magnificence danced various shades of green and blue across the sky. I'd never realized how beautiful they were. In fact, I hadn't fully appreciated the splendour of nature on Earth as I did this day, now.

I knew when I fell asleep my past life would unfold; the very thought filled me with apprehension. I mustered up all the tenacity within me to keep my eyes open, but it was in vain. My eyelids grew heavier and heavier and finally closed.

6

Virginia Rail

Jonathan Brown walked into the restaurant and scanned the room, looking for the familiar face of his cousin, Michael Smith. Michael, the only relative his age, had played a large role in his life, only to move away and return ten years later when they'd grown into young men. It hadn't taken long for the cousins to pick up the missing years and become the best of friends once again.

The aroma of fresh coffee and bacon filled the atmosphere where a small collection of patrons enjoyed their breakfast. The song "My Way" played overhead. It didn't take long for Jonathan's searching eyes to find Michael. He sat at the far end of the room, impatiently drumming his fingers on the table. When their eyes met, he broke out in a large grin, a trait Jonathan always found appealing. He smiled back. This weekly visit with his cousin was a special time—a break from the daily routine of the bank and family.

"Hello, my man. How goes it?" asked Michael.

"Well, I've been busy signing up the boys for midget hockey for the fall. You know they've been playing ball all summer and are getting close to the playoffs. Now that they're fifteen, they need sports to settle down those damn, raging hormones. Sports is the best thing for kids, I think. It might have been good for me too, instead of piano. But I must admit, piano was a release."

His latter statement rolled Jonathan's thoughts back to his childhood, when he'd let the air out of the tires of the neighbours' new car and how he'd drawn comfort by ceaselessly pounding the ivories that fateful day. He could still feel the sting from the memory.

"I agree," said Michael. "By the way, you remember last week when I told you about the purchase I was trying to close? Well, it's in the bag; the deal is cinched. It brings the total of my hotels to fifteen. I'm still looking for a charity to contribute to—need to cut back on my personal taxes, you know, or I'll really get hammered."

"You can't go wrong with supporting sports. There's always a need for that, and besides, you'll be helping out your second cousins, or is it first cousins, once removed?" He gave Michael a wink, hoping he'd inveigled him.

Plates of bacon and eggs were set before them and they hungrily devoured their breakfast while touching on many subjects of mutual interest. After several minutes, they stood up, gave each other a high five, and agreed to meet again next month.

Jonathan arose early this Sunday morning to prepare for his nature walk in the woods with his fifteen-year-old twin sons. Being able to catch them in between sporting activities had become a rarity. He packed bottles of water, some leftover dinner rolls, a chunk of cheese, and three bright, red McIntosh apples. And last, most importantly, the binoculars.

A naturalist by heart, he enjoyed nothing more than the smell of the earth and the crunch beneath his feet of last year's forestation warming the forest floor. Most of all, it would be a pleasure to point out his favourite water bird, the Virginia rail, to Jimmy and Robert, his sons, and listen for its variety of calls, some unrecognizable but foremost the rather loud, kicker call that was erroneously only attributed for years to its cousin, the yellow rail.

"What do they sound like, Dad?" asked Jimmy, the younger of the twins by two minutes. Pleased by the interest, his father replied.

"They have a large variety of calls. I think sometimes it sounds like a cross between a cackle and a bark. Hey, did you just hear that? It sounded close. Shh, shh, let's see if we can find it."

He raised the binoculars and scanned the trees, but to no avail. The call came again. It seemed lower down this time. Jonathan scanned the marshes and to his delight spotted one of his favourite birds feeding.

"Here, have a look." He passed the binoculars to his sons to share.

"Wow, it sure has a long beak!" said Jimmy. "I like his nice brown colour!" said Robert.

"Sons, now that you've seen the Virginia rail, let me tell you something about these amazing birds. They live in marshes across this continent, eating insects and larvae. They poke that long beak into the mud or shallow water to forage for food, or they pick insects off plants that grow in the marsh."

Rules For Living On Earth

"Cool!" said Robert.

"Where do they build their nests?" asked Jimmy.

"In a dry area of the marsh or on shallow water, usually in a dense clump of vegetation. Both the male and female build the nest."

"What do they use?"

"They use cattails, reeds, and grasses. They build it under a canopy of living plants for protection. That way they cannot be seen too quickly. Both male and female build the nest."

"What colour are their eggs?"

"They're a light buff colour with a dark speckling of brown and grey."

He could see his answers were pleasing his sons.

"Who feeds the chicks?"

"They both do, just like they build their nest. They do things together. Quite a partnership! The chicks become independent at about three weeks old and can fly at twenty-five days old. Pretty amazing facts about the Virginia rail, I'd say."

"Sure is, Dad!" the boys exclaimed together.

"Now you know why it's my favourite bird. But it's a sad thing that their habitats are being eaten up by mankind and their developments."

The Browns finished their little Sunday excursion by going to McDonald's for their favourite burgers and fries. Jonathan was happy to have had this nature time with his sons.

They're growing so fast, I wish I could do this more often. I want them to appreciate nature, he thought as he pulled the car into the driveway.

Two weeks passed and with the summer sports winding down, Jonathan decided to drive past Mason's Marsh on his way home from the bank. He did a double-take, pulled over to the side of the road, and slammed on his brakes. He couldn't fathom what he was seeing! A bulldozer was ripping through the end of the marsh, piling up debris and pushing the muddy collection to the side of the road.

"This can't be happening; they're destroying the wetland, the home of the Virginia rail. How can they do such a thing?" he declared aloud. "The numbskulls!"

He jumped out of his car and ran toward the bulldozer, flailing his arms and losing a shoe in the newly unearthed mud in the process.

"Stop! he shouted. "Stop!"

The big machine came to a grinding halt.

"What do you think you're doing?" he continued to shout. "You're destroying the marsh."

The dozer operator jumped down and walked over to him.

"I'm doing my job. Who the hell are you?"

Jonathan, panting from his exertion, ignored his question. "Who hired you to do this … this terrible thing?"

"The city did, I'll have you know. What's it to ya, mister?"

"Wild fowl depend on this marsh. You've probably destroyed nesting sites already. I'm heading to the city right now to put a stop to it."

After retrieving his shoe from the mud, he drove to City Hall. Dark mud covered the front of his suit, and his wet shoe made a sucking sound as he walked swiftly up to the receptionist.

"Do you have an appointment?" she asked, smiling sweetly at the dishevelled man.

"No, I don't," he replied impatiently.

"Can I have your name please, sir?"

"Jonathan Brown—now please get the mayor; this is an emergency!"

"Okay, okay, please don't shout at me." She walked swiftly to the back of the room and disappeared through a doorway.

He regretted raising his voice. He knew how disgusted he felt when clients did the same to the tellers in the bank.

You can bet right at this moment she's complaining to the mayor.

A few minutes later, a short, balding man with a no-nonsense look on his face walked heavy-footed and swiftly to the counter, raising a few papers on the corner desk as he passed.

"What can I do for you, Mr. Brown?" His voice was remarkably deep for his stature. He noticed the dishevelled man before him with mud on his suit.

Jonathan ignored the hand the mayor had extended. He wasn't in the mood for niceties.

"You can put a stop to the carnage that's occurring at Mason's Marsh!"

"And what exactly would that be?" queried the mayor as he shifted from one foot to the other.

"A bulldozer ripping out half the bloody marsh, that's what! You, as mayor, must be aware of that."

"If you're talking about the land prep for the new ball diamond, of course I'm aware. It came before council last week and was passed unanimously."

"Did you give any consideration to the water fowl and other creatures that depend on the marsh? No, of course you didn't, for if you had, you wouldn't be doing it."

Jonathan didn't give the mayor a chance to reply. He kept on talking, his voice growing louder with each word.

"Why couldn't you put the ball diamond in the empty field by the recreation centre? That would have made a whole lot more sense. I'm going to put a stop to this travesty. And you can bet I won't be voting for you next time round. You are the closest thing to an ignoramus I've ever met!"

Jonathan turned on his heel, leaving the mayor speechless and all of the clerks whispering to each other. By the time he reached his vehicle, his temper had come down. He chastised himself for calling the mayor an ignoramus and contemplated going back in to apologize.

No. Why should I apologize? He should be apologizing to the city for ruining the home of the Virginia rail and other birds and animals. No, I won't go back in.

Instead, as he drove home he hatched a plan for revenge. Later that night, three hours before daylight with his household deep in sleep, he quietly left his home.

I felt a push on my shoulder and awoke with the hammock gently swinging back and forth. I could feel the warmth of the morning sun on my face and could hear the chirping of many birds. When I opened my eyes, there, bigger than life, was David looking down over me and smiling. I was hoping I hadn't died after all and that these stations of reckoning were merely a dream, but alas, that was not the case. Seeing David again and feeling his nudge was a sure sign that this was my new reality. The frustration I felt over the destruction of the marsh lingered with me, and I knew I would have to answer for the revenge I took those early morning hours.

"Welcome back," said David. "Come walk with me; we have to talk."

I left the hammock and fell into a gliding stride with David. The path was just wide enough for the two of us. I walked slowly beside him, drinking in the beauty of nature all around us at its most superlative. It seemed a long time before he spoke.

"You are commended for showing concern for the inhabitants of the all-important wetlands. But in showing your disapproval, you broke two other rules for living on Earth. You were extremely rude and unkind to the mayor, and filling up the bulldozer's tank in the middle of the night with twenty pounds of sugar was an act of vandalism. Both of these acts negate the benefits for showing concern for the preservation of the wetlands."

His words hit me like a bolt of lightning. We continued on in silence. After much thought, I realized my folly. Not at first, of course. At first I argued with myself that I'd been justified, but now I was sorry—very sorry—for my behaviour. Remorse increased with each step I took. He must have sensed my regret, for he turned toward me, flashed a smile, and tweaked my shoulder. He began to speak again, and I dreaded what I might hear.

"However, Jonathan, there are two things that have tipped the scale in your favour."

In my favour? Did I hear correctly?

Relief washed over me like a cool shower on a hot day.

"What are these two things?" I asked.

"Number one is when you so gallantly stood up at the recycling forum and defended the necessity of it, and number two is when you took your sons to the marsh and instilled in them the value of the marsh and gave them a lesson on the Virginia rail. A fine lesson for one of nature's fine little birds, I might add."

I realized then that he knew everything about me … absolutely everything. The very thought made me cringe inside. I caught my breath.

Humbly I whispered, "What I did was so little, almost nothing that could possibly matter."

He stopped and turned to me, a stern countenance replacing his usually smiling face.

"Jonathan, if every person, or even one in ten, did something to preserve nature, the Earth would be preserved, so to speak. At present, streams are full of poisonous chemicals from industrial processes, rivers are overloaded from farm fertilizers, and skies are filled with smog. All of these can affect a landscape as far away as a thousand miles. If everyone did their bit, mankind would not be suffering from diseases, and we wouldn't find dead sea creatures washing up on shores. Whales and dolphins have beached in protest, but man is too naïve to recognize their reason."

His voice became husky, and I could tell he had more to say.

"The Earth and all of its splendour and life thereupon, with all of its intricacies, is a gift from the Creator. Life itself is a gift. How could anyone doubt that? What more proof do they need? God has given man a brain to think scientifically to investigate the origin of the universe and has allowed him to unravel a small part of creation to a point where man in his arrogance has begun to question the reality of the Creator, known to us as God."

A chuckle rose from deep in his throat. He threw his head back and declared, "Man simply does not understand that the scientific discoveries he makes are merely a test of faith."

He continued talking as we moved down the path. The scenery around began to change, and the beauty of nature began to dissipate. I could see the gate ahead.

David stopped and turned to me. "This is the end of my jurisdiction, where I must say goodbye."

He extended his hand and I accepted his exuberant handshake; it made me feel appreciated. I found myself at a loss for words. All I could think of saying was, "Thank you."

A robin sat atop the post that held the hinges of the gate. It fluttered its wings as if to say goodbye. I wondered if it was the same robin that had greeted me earlier. I believed it was. The creaking sound of the gate swinging open caused it to fly away. Once again, I was moved down a lonely path that was long and winding. I tried to see where it ended, but in vain; it seemingly was without end. I appeared to be moving somewhat faster this time, but with many thoughts bouncing back and forth like a ball in a racquet court.

I thought about how David, in all his simplicity, had been sitting there on the rock when I arrived. He was smiling amidst the beauty of nature like he owned it. The unwavering smile left a strong impact upon me, as did his soft voice speaking ever so factually. Why had he led me to a hammock for the replay of my life as it pertained to the rule of protecting the Earth? I supposed it was better than capturing me behind a tree relieving myself. My base thought left me embarrassed. I scolded myself.

Yes, David left an impact upon me alright—so much so I now questioned everything I'd taken for granted. The beauty of David's Earth and the one I'd left behind was like an orchestra playing to my thoughts. How could anything be so beautiful, so exact, if not for a Supreme Being? How could a juicy apple spring forth from a tree branch, or a red rose come out of dark soil? How could any of it occur, including the creation of new life, without a master-mind behind it all? I was forced to look at my atheism. How could I change what I'd held so staunchly for so long?

Much to my consternation, just when I thought I was moving more quickly onto the next rule, I began to slow down. And what would that next rule be? I began to analyze myself, analyze how I'd lived my life on Earth. I knew there would have to be a reckoning. I began to feel a deep shame as I remembered certain aspects of my life—especially Rosalyn. Oh yes … Rosalyn, my faithful little mistress, who for the past three years had always been there to provide a soft, warm place for me to land. I'd met her at the annual bank audit. She'd been fresh out of college and oozed sex appeal. Her sly glances in my direction had told me I had a chance with her, a younger woman to stroke my ego. I'd given in to infidelity for no other reason than simply because I could. Not once did I question how I was interrupting Rosalyn's life … how I was holding her back from normalcy.

But what about Gina, the mother of my twin sons, the woman who has stood by me through all circumstances over the years, the one who nurtured my sons, attended all

of the school meetings, who never questioned anything I told her, like the weekly and frequent late meetings at the bank
while, in fact, I was cozening under the
covers with Rosalyn? Yes, my treatment
of Gina deepened my shame as I was moved
through the fog down the lonely road with
dark mist all around me. Then the odour of
fish, decaying fish left in a boat in the
hot sun for days, surrounded me and left
me gagging. It matched the dread that had
engulfed me—so much dread, in fact, that
I couldn't entertain another thought.

7

The Test

After what seemed an eternity, the odour left and the fog parted, exposing a two-storey building with many reflective windows giving an all-around mirror effect. It reminded me of one of the banks I'd superintended on Earth.

I was moved up a multitude of steps to the front door, which sprang open in front of me, exposing a long hallway carpeted in a mosaic pattern of leaves in various colours. At the end of the hall an elderly, grey-haired gentleman sat behind a large oak desk, writing in a notebook. I was placed on a chair in front of him. He kept busily writing and didn't look up, but I knew he was aware of me.

As time passed I wondered how long I would have to wait. Everything on this trip was a test of my patience. I was growing more uncomfortable by the minute. At long last he snapped his notebook shut, opened a drawer, and withdrew a bronze placard. He placed it in the middle of his desk and turned it around so I could see it. One word was emblazoned in capital letters across its middle.

His piercing blue eyes met mine.

"My name is Mark," he said, "and I'm in charge of the station for Honesty." He pointed his finger to the word on the placard.

"I'm Jonathan Brown," I said.

"I know exactly who you are." He smiled. "And to be honest," he pointed once again to the word, "I must warn you that I know everything about you, Jonathan—absolutely everything you did on Earth. I know when you blew your nose. You and I have to have a long talk."

I felt exposed, naked, and vulnerable, and I knew there was much I would have to explain—or try to deny. I grabbed at my inner being to find some courage, some dignity, with just a small measure of success.

"I've always been an honest man," I proclaimed. I hoped he didn't know about some of things I'd done; perhaps he was kidding about knowing everything.

"Let's start with your denial of letting the air out of the tires on the Cadillac. That wasn't honest."

"I was only fourteen years old, for goodness' sake."

"You were at an age of reason; age is no excuse. Now, we have a lot of ground to cover, so let's move on," said Mark. "I know you managed to graduate high school with fairly good grades, but did you achieve them honestly?"

"What do you mean, did I achieve them honestly? Of course I did. Are you insinuating I cheated?"

"Jonathan, are you forgetting I know everything about you? You cannot deny anything in your life."

"What is it I'm denying now?"

"Allow me to refresh your memory. Remember when you were about to write your history exam? Two days before you complained to your mother that history was the stupidest subject you'd ever taken, that finding out about what happened hundreds of years ago had no bearing on your life, so you refused to study? However, when you went to school the next day, you realized that you needed to pass the exam to attain the necessary credits to graduate. Now do you remember?"

I could feel my face flush as it all came rushing back to me.

"I barely remember; it was so long ago."

"Well," said Mark with a sigh, "the next day you went to school and you stayed after school, flipping and scanning the pages of your history book while the teacher worked on preparing the exam for the next day. She was called out of the room for a few minutes. When she was gone, you went up to her desk and took pictures of each page with your cell phone and then quickly left for home. You emailed them to yourself and enlarged them onto your computer screen. You were able to read ninety per cent of the questions and memorized the answers. The next day, when all of the students were busy writing, you finished early and turned in your paper. Your teacher thought you'd finished quickly because she'd witnessed you studying the day before. She smiled broadly at you. Tell me, Jonathan, do you think that was being honest?"

The full memory was with me now. I felt guilty and ashamed. "No, Mark, it wasn't being honest. I cheated."

Mark gave me a long accusatory stare, as though he could see into my innermost self. I was cringing when he continued.

"Let's move on. You worked in a bank and eventually became a bank manager. Did you achieve this position entirely in an honest way?"

I hesitated to answer in case he proved me wrong.

"Yes, I did. I worked long and hard to get there, I'll have you know."

I chastised myself for sounding cheeky. Hadn't he said he knew everything about me? I waited with bated breath for his reply.

"Jonathan, there were three of you vying for the position of manager. You pointed out the weaknesses of your competitors as often as you could during the prior year. You even started a rumour about your strongest competitor to darken his chances. It paid off for you, didn't it? You landed the position. You even shook the hands of your two adversaries, wishing them well and saying, 'Your turn is coming.'"

I couldn't believe my ears. Actually, I'd forgotten about all of those details. I couldn't deny it. Everything he said was true. To say I felt terrible about it all was an understatement. I was humiliated and so sorry about it all.

Recognizing my regret, he said, "I see you're sorry."

I nodded and hung my head.

"There's one more segment we need to deal with, as it pertains to honesty. I think this is the most grievous of all."

I wondered what could possibly be next.

He stood up, walked over to the window, and opened it as if to let all of the bad air out. He turned abruptly around.

Helpless, I watched him as he began to speak in a stern voice.

"You married a beautiful woman."

"Yes, I surely did."

"She gave you twin sons who are now in college."

"Yes, she surely did."

I sounded like a broken record and felt silly. I was sure I knew where he was heading.

"Were you always honest with this beautiful woman who gave you twin sons?"

He'd backed me into a corner. I felt trapped.

"I believe, sir, you know the answer."

He looked me in the eye and nodded. I saw his face soften as he became cognizant of my shame, my repentance, which had come spontaneously.

My voice was hoarse when I uttered, "I wish I could change all of that. I'd give anything if I could."

A few minutes of silence followed. My head hung in shame and regret.

Breaking the silence, he continued, "I do have to compliment you on the many times you lectured your sons, and also the bank employees, about being honest. You coined the old phrase, 'Honesty is always the best policy.' Your behaviour was the classic example of another old phrase, 'Do as I say, not as I do.'"

He smiled at me for the first time. I felt a measure of relief.

"Well, Jonathan, the time has come for you to move on. You have come through the rules of Envy, Prejudice, Taking Care of the Earth, and now Honesty. Yes, it's time for you to move on."

"Can I ask you a question?" I pleaded.

"By all means," replied Mark.

"How many more stations do I have to reach? And then what?"

"I have some good news for you. You have only one more station to reach. It's the very last station, and I have to say, the most important station of all! That's all I can tell you. Now follow me."

He clearly wasn't about to tell me more. He stood up and opened the door, and I followed him out into the hallway. Taking a turn to the right, I was propelled toward a long, winding staircase. I turned to say goodbye. He wished me good luck and immediately swung around to leave. I didn't know if he heard me say, "Thank you."

8

Sebastian

As I climbed, my body miraculously came back to me. No longer was I moving like a phantom with no control over my movements. I wondered if this entire scenario was a dream. Could it be a dream? If so, whose bed would I wake up in—my wife's, or Rosalyn's? More importantly, would I remember all that had transpired? Some of my dreams in the past just slipped away from my mind into thin air the moment I woke up. I thought once again about the stations I'd passed through, their keepers, and how my trips back to Earth had given me shame and regret. I recalled how the station about prejudice was so graphically displayed with human innards, it made me feel like I'd been dragged through a ditch of slough water.

Continuing to move upwards, I had mixed emotions. On one hand, I was happy to know I was about to reach my last station, while on the other, I was apprehensive as to what it would be. Most of all, and the biggest mystery, was what lay beyond. I reminded myself that I didn't believe in God, but now, overcome with worry, my atheistic armour began to lose a little of its shine.

I shrugged it off and told myself, *Buck up, Jonathan. After all you've been through, what could possibly daunt you now?* I kept climbing up, up, up … one step after another. I looked up and could see no end. My legs felt like they were weighted down with lead, and the muscles in my knees felt nonexistent. Finally, fatigue took over and I collapsed onto the steps. I lay across the sharp corners of the steps and could feel painful pressure cutting into my rib cage. I knew if I tried to stand, I would topple down. I lay there in agony. Then, to my relief, I heard a gentle voice saying, "I'll help you, Jonathan; you're almost there. Here, take my hand. I'll help you up."

I looked up into the kindly face of a red-haired man who couldn't be any older than twenty. I gratefully took the hand he offered. He put his arm across my shoulders to support me.

"Thank you," I mumbled, the words barely audible.

He encouraged me further in a soft voice, which was music to my ears. "Just a few more steps. You can do it."

With his help, we climbed together, one foot in front of the other, up, up, up. At long last, we arrived at the top where there was a closed door. In the middle of this pristine, white door with its sparkling, gold knob were the words: LOVE AND KINDNESS. Despite my weakened condition, I understood: the shimmering gold lettering indicated I was going to be privy to something special, something very special, that lay beyond. He opened the door and we entered.

My hair was ringing wet, and I could feel perspiration dripping down my back. My legs still felt like they were weighted down. I was guided to a bed and I fell upon it. Sleep overtook me before I could find out who the young man was.

I didn't know how long I slept; time had no significance. All I knew was that I felt wonderfully refreshed when I awoke. I sat up. There beside my bed stood the young man who had helped me. I was first to speak.

"How can I thank you for being so kind to me? I could never have made it up the stairs without you. My name is Jonathan. What's yours, and what's your job here?"

He gave me an easy smile. "I'm Sebastian. I guess you might call me your personal assistant, your valet, so to speak. We have a busy day ahead of us. First, I'm sure you would like to shower. Over in the closet are clothes and several pairs of shoes you can choose from, and in the dresser drawer next to it are socks and underwear. The shower and toilet are over there."

He nodded at a door just left of the bed. "When you're finished, you can join me in the dining room down the hall." He turned and left the room.

The shower was glorious against my tired skin, and I lingered there for quite a spell. I was amazed at the clothes in the closet; they appeared to have been shipped up from my closet on Earth. I chose pale-blue jeans and a matching flannel shirt. The bathroom held my toiletries, and by the time I finished dressing, brushing my teeth, and combing my hair, I was ravenous and ready to walk down the hall to the dining room, which I hoped meant food. I gave a glance of approval in the full-length mirror on the bathroom door before I left.

As I walked to the dining room, I resolutely made up my mind to get to the bottom of my situation once and for all. I needed to know my whereabouts and what lay ahead. This time I would demand some definitive answers to my bizarre situation. I was washed and groomed, and once I'd eaten, I would be ready for action. I thought about how royally I was being treated and the kindness being shown to me. I supposed the powers that be were living up to the "Love and Kindness" slogan that was blazing on the front door. But that didn't daunt me. I wasn't going to be deterred from my quest for answers.

As I approached the dining room entrance, the pungent aroma of tomato and garlic filled my nostrils. I began to salivate. How did they know pasta was my all-time favourite?

Sebastian was there to greet me. He smiled warmly and said, "Welcome, Jonathan, I see you're all freshened up and ready for your day. Come along with me and let's enjoy a meal together. There will be a number of folks you'll have to meet once we've eaten."

We sat down at a circular table covered with a white cloth. The napkins placed beside our gold-rimmed, white dinner plates were a soft yellow, and the cutlery a sparkling gold. Daisies of every colour overflowed in a flat bowl in the middle of the table. A bottle of Merlot stood between the two plates. I'd attended many fancy dinners put on by various banks around the world, but nothing compared to this. As I sat appreciating the decor, I was treated to soft music playing in the background; a collection of my favourite concertos created ambiance like no other.

A man in a white jacket walked in balancing a tantalizing steaming platter of meat balls and spaghetti smothered with tomato sauce in one hand, and in the other, a platter of crusty garlic bread. He placed both on the table in front of us, then poured the wine into the two goblets at our setting. I ate with gusto. Sebastian had bowed his head, closed his eyes, and silently given a prayer of thanks before he touched his food. Much to my surprise, I felt like an ingrate, but at the moment I didn't care. I was hungry. Besides, I didn't believe in all that gobbledygook.

Once we'd wiped our mouths with our napkins, I was ready to talk. I took a swallow of my wine and spoke first.

"Once again, Sebastian, I'd like to thank you for all the courtesy you've shown me. I do have some questions that need answering, though."

He didn't show any surprise. "Ask away."

"Well … Where am I? I recall being hit by a truck and floating upward. I've passed through several stations, which I understand are some kind of rules for living on Earth, and that this place is the last. Is that so?"

"First of all, Jonathan, you're in the space between Earth and Heaven, and yes, this is your last station."

"And who are you, Sebastian? Who are you? Really?"

"As I told you before, I'm your guide, and I'm also your friend. I've volunteered to do this job. Like you, I was once on Earth. I worked several years as a social worker until I suffered an illness that took me to the Creator. Some people like to think of me as their guardian angel. I have to admit it makes me feel pretty good when I hear this."

He gave me another of his warm smiles and a wink.

"I'm sorry to say, Sebastian, but I think that's a lot of bunk."

"I know you do, and that's why you're here."

"Why I'm here? What's that supposed to mean?"

"You're here for a reason, Jonathan. It isn't just a happenstance. You're here to learn. Some people come here because, when on Earth, they were never taught about the Creator, never had the chance. The tougher challenge are the others who were taught when they were young, but when they got older, decided they knew better, had all the answers, and considered the facts told were just a lot of bunk—as you put it."

"You say I'm here to learn. How exactly is that going to happen?"

"We're going to go into a large living room where you will meet a number of people … people whose main goal is to teach you about Love and Kindness. They're all experts in their field. I guess one could call them professors. There will be a question and answer period. You'll be able to ask all the questions you want, and you're guaranteed to get answers. You will be able to examine your life on Earth in relation to the topic. No one will be blaming you for anything; they'll just be trying to help you understand the subject at hand. Actually, it's a beautiful thing. You'll see."

"What *are* the subjects, the topics? I'm very interested to know."

"Well, let me see. It all comes under the umbrella of 'Love and Kindness,' which includes greed, gluttony, conceit, justice, grudging, fairness, consideration, respect, degradation, arrogance, compassion, and humility."

He caught his breath and continued, "These subjects are just a few and are merely titles with subtitles beneath them. There's much for you to learn."

"You can say that again. Sounds like a full glass of water to me."

Sebastian threw his head back and laughed at the analogy.

"So let's head off into the living room now and meet these kind folks," he said. "Just follow me."

9

Esther

We walked into a large, warmly-lit living room. There was a head table with two chairs, and, to my surprise, Sebastian guided me there. We sat down. I gazed around the room at an arc of chairs surrounding our table, occupied by men and women of all ages. They looked so pleasant and happy, like they were having a great time. The atmosphere was gentle, if one could describe it that way. I wondered if they too were angels. They were smiling with their eyes upon me. I could tell they were anxious to get busy with the subject at hand: me. I didn't feel threatened. Actually, I was getting a bit of a hoot out of it all. I hoped when I woke up from this dream I would remember all of it.

A middle-aged, dark-haired lady in a simple, white, long-sleeved dress with navy collar and cuffs stepped forward from the group. Apparently, she was the Master of Ceremonies. She smiled at me and said, "My name is Esther."

I nodded and said, "And mine is Jonathan Brown."

She whispered, "I know."

She raised her voice and announced, "Ladies and gentlemen, it is my profound pleasure to introduce our guest of honour, Jonathan Brown. You all know his guide, Sebastian."

A roar of applause followed. I felt I should stand up and take a bow but thought better of it.

Directing her attention back to me, she continued.

"Welcome, Jonathan, to this, your final station: Love and Kindness. Love and Kindness is a tree with many branches. We will address them today. Love and Kindness hold the secret to all that is good on Earth—all that will, if understood and acknowledged, take you to the Creator."

"Yes!" The echo of approval resonated around the room. Even Sebastian, who sat stoically by my side, cheered.

"And Jonathan," she continued, "if at any time you have a question, please raise your hand."

That was all I needed; my hand shot up. "I do have a question. What's all this rhetoric about there being a Creator? Many people on Earth believe the planet is part of an immense universe with innumerable millions of galaxies that has always existed. There's no 'Creator,' so to speak." I made air quotes with my fingers when saying, "Creator." "They also believe there are other forms of life on other planets."

Esther replied, "Those are common beliefs expressed by the people who come to this station. They also believe the Earth was created by the Big Bang theory, which is an attempt to explain how the universe developed from a very tiny, dense state to what it is today. As far as life on other planets is concerned, despite a lot of research in outer space, scientists have not yet been allowed to find evidence of life forms on any other planet besides Earth."

"That's true," I replied. "The Big Bang theory seems to make a lot more sense to me."

Esther smiled and said, "Well, Sebastian, it looks like you have to make a choice between a Supreme Creator on one hand or the Big Bang theory on the other." She emphasized the word "bang."

I heard a soft snicker ripple through the audience. She made it seem so simple, so easily understood, so elementary, so juvenile. I could think of nothing else to say. The phrase "make a choice" kept ringing in my ears. It gave me food for thought, but not for a moment did it dissuade me from my own beliefs.

"Let's move on with our program," said Esther, smiling. She gazed around at the people in the arc of chairs. "Who would like to start?"

An elderly gentleman with a grey beard came forward and Esther took his seat. When he stood at the podium, he smiled, looked at me, and said, "Hello, Jonathan, my name's Walter. The Creator has asked me to speak today in this Love and Kindness forum."

The assembly gave a round of applause, which he acknowledged with a nod and a whisper. "Thank you. For many years, I was a stock broker on Earth, and I have chosen the subject of greed. Actually, greed is my speciality. I say 'speciality' because I think I was the greediest person who ever lived on the face of the Earth! Wouldn't you say that qualifies me for this part of our little forum?" He smiled at everyone.

I found myself nodding, anxious to hear more.

"Please interject anytime you wish. You and I can dialogue together along with anyone else who wants to join in.

"I amassed a fortune on Earth, but having a fortune was never enough. I hoarded money. If I gave anything to charity, it was purely for tax purposes and never with a charitable heart. Even as a youngster, I always had to have the biggest piece of the pie, and somehow I always managed to get it, not caring who I hurt along the way. As I grew older, I did whatever it took …yes, Jonathan?" He acknowledged my raised hand.

"What's wrong with keeping what one works hard to earn?"

"There's nothing wrong with keeping what we earn, but remember, if you keep more than what you need with no regard to the hardship of others, that is greed and certainly not kindness to other humans less fortunate than yourself. As I was saying, I did whatever it took, not caring whose toes I stepped on."

I rested my chin in the palm of my hand, listening intently to Walter and thinking about who I'd bumped out of my way.

He continued, "Having a new Lincoln in my possession wasn't enough. I had to have two Lincolns in different colours, a Jaguar, a white Cadillac, a Lamborghini, and a variety of small sports cars. I paid no heed to the young family who didn't own one car, waiting at the bus stop in pouring rain so they could get their groceries."

I jumped to my feet and blurted, "We can't be responsible for other people's dilemmas. Some people are damn lazy and just don't want to work."

"We have to remember, Jonathan, that not everyone has been given the same opportunities in life. They're less fortunate financially, they don't have the opportunity for a higher education, while others have a poor spirit without the internal drive to get ahead. Altogether just less fortunate all the way around. We must remember this. Greed is a terrible, terrible thing, leaving one without the empathy you've just now expressed."

I sat down feeling angry and somewhat deflated. Sebastian, who had been sitting motionless beside me, reached over and patted my hand, which I recognized as encouragement. To show him his action wasn't in vain, I posed the question, "What causes greed?"

"Self-doubt, negative feelings, psychological addiction, and excessive longing for wealth and possessions mistakenly believed to increase self worth. The greedy person lacks wisdom and, more importantly, Jonathan, they lack love and kindness."

After making the last emphatic statement, he nodded to Esther that he was finished. He'd made his point most effectively. The audience applauded as he walked back to his seat. The smile on his face wasn't one of arrogance, but of achievement.

I had to admit … he had me thinking and asking myself: *Was I greedy in my life? Did I lack sympathy?* I scratched my brain, thinking about whether or not I was. The odds told me I was. Many incidents flashed across my mind proving that point. I felt ashamed and regretful. I wished I could return to Earth and relive those times to make them right.

I watched Esther come back to the podium, wondering what would be next and what would happen when this forum was finished. The not knowing was the most frustrating part of this dream I felt certain was happening. I wished I would wake up.

"Thank you, Walter, that was an excellent talk on greed. As I said before, the tree of Love and Kindness has many branches. I know all of you are here on a special mission for our all-important subject. This special mission is for you, Jonathan."

She beamed a smile in my direction. I knew her intention was to make me feel important and it did … a little.

"Who would like to speak next?"

I heard a stir at the far left of the arc of seats. A young woman in a sky-blue, slim-fitting dress was walking toward the podium. As she walked up to the front, her long, golden hair flowed down her back. She was of average height and as shapely as any model could ever hope to be. I was anxious for her to turn around so that I could see her face. Wow! I was mesmer-ized. Large, sparkling-blue eyes beamed toward me. Her round face and a complex-ion underscoring the expression of peach-es and cream were further complemented by a pert, turned-up nose and flashing white teeth. She was the prettiest woman I'd ever laid my eyes upon. I was anxious to hear her speak.

"Hello, Jonathan, my name's Ann. The Creator requested I speak on the subject, 'Conceit.'"

How appropriate, I thought. Her voice surprised me. I'd expected it to be soft and sweet; in fact, it was low-pitched and husky.

She continued, "Like Walter, who at the beginning of his speech said he was the greediest person who'd ever lived on Earth, I, without a doubt, was the most conceited. From as far back as I can remember, I knew I was beautiful. As a child, people stopped my parents on the street so they could have a closer look at me. In school, fellow students lined up to be my friend. As I grew up, I couldn't pass a mirror without looking into it. I think the song "You're So Vain" could have been written about me. I was so in love with myself, nothing else and nobody else mattered. I even took a mirror to bed so I could gaze upon my face should I awaken. At an early age, I knew my beauty would get me anything I wanted, and I used it. Boy, did I use it! Then one day I came to my senses. I was diagnosed with cancer.

"During my time in the hospital, the process of chemotherapy and the excellent, loving care I received made me realize that true beauty comes from within. I say that because the nurse assigned to my care was a homely woman. Her nose was too big, her eyes were too small, and her skin was swarthy. At first I found it hard to look at her. Later when she attended to me, I felt the loving care she was giving me—her gentle hands, soft voice, kind eyes, good nature, and all-around sweetness. It was then I realized she was a truly beautiful person!

"And I realized the outside of one's self is only window dressing. It's the inside of a person that really counts. I thought about how unkind and unloving I'd been to others in the past—judging them by their exterior, not looking for the goodness within them. Oh, how wrong I was! How conceited and blind I'd been!"

I sat mesmerized by what she was saying. There was no question to ask. Again, I was filled with despair when I thought about all of the people I'd judged wrongly, judged merely by their appearance without looking further. What a huge mistake I'd made.

Ann continued, "Well, Jonathan, that's really all I have to say. Oh, one more thing: if one's heart is filled with love and kindness, there's absolutely no room for conceit and arrogance. I hope you understand what I mean."

I couldn't help nod and smile at her as she walked back to her chair. I'd always known character to be more important than appearance, but if I'd had any doubt whatsoever, this beautiful creature certainly made it emphatically clear. She had a talent for holding one's attention.

I turned to Sebastian and whispered, "She's beautiful … very beautiful."

Sebastian replied, "Moreover, she's very nice." He made his point.

I raised my hand to ask a question.

Esther nodded.

"Something else that has really puzzled me on Earth is prayer. I've witnessed how so many people flock into churches to, I assume, pray. I think there are so many hypocrites among them that are just wanting to be seen. I believe they think it helps them in their business to wear a sanctimonious cap once a week, while the rest of the week they cheat and steal. I think this prayer thing is just a bunch of senseless mumbo jumbo, especially those who profess to be able to pray in tongues. I want to know what this so-called God of yours thinks about prayer. Does he ever answer a prayer? Does he answer a prayer to save a life? Are you able to answer me that?

"And what about those people on Earth who go from church to church? I've heard them say they just weren't getting anything out of the church. They didn't like the minister. It just didn't do anything for them spiritually, so they would try another one. Praying in a church didn't seem to work for them. What do you have to say about that?"

I fell back into my chair, making a plopping sound as if to put more emphasis on my question.

Esther spoke quickly. "Of course we're able." She nodded to the middle row. "Gordon, would you like to address that subject?"

The man she'd addressed was instantly on his feet. "I'd be happy to, ma'am."

His silver hair, in contrast to the black blazer he wore, appeared to sparkle as he walked up to the microphone with an air of dignity. I noticed that his handsome countenance showed experience, and his eyes, wisdom. I was amazed at how tall the man was and guessed him to be at least six-foot-five. His deep voice thundered throughout the room.

"First of all, only our Creator knows what lies in the hearts and minds of a person when attending church, and only He can be the judge. We must remember, however, that the church is not an entertainment centre. It's a place to communicate with God. When a group of people gather to honour God, He is right there with them. If it's entertainment that's wanted, there are plenty of venues for that; for example, the theatre."

His last remark drew soft giggles from the audience.

"God considers every prayer that is offered to Him. He will not answer your prayer right away or at all if your request is not within His will. He has other plans for you. I repeat, prayers are answered all according to God's will."

I sat speechless at his logical words emitted in that deep, baritone voice.

"I would like to tell you," continued Gordon, "about something that happened to me on Earth."

He coughed and cleared his throat. The importance of what he was about to say demanded clarity of tone.

"I was a die-heart atheist who never prayed, never believed in prayer, and swore I would never pray. Then one day I was panic-stricken, thinking something had happened to my wife.

"We'd made a trip to a large city to buy another vehicle. For the return trip, I drove the new vehicle, and she drove the family car. She'd consistently told me she wasn't comfortable driving in the dark. The conclusion of the sale was taking longer than anticipated, and dusk was closing in. To make matters worse, it was pouring rain. She was to follow me, and we were to meet at the ferry terminal.

"After several miles, I noticed she wasn't behind me and assumed she must be a few cars back. I arrived first and expected her to arrive shortly after, but she didn't. Many minutes went by, which turned into an hour. I was sure something bad … very bad … had happened to my new wife, who was the love of my life.

"I tried phoning her on her cell, but there was no reply. I was panic stricken! My back was against the wall. I didn't know what to do or what to think. In my desperation, I decided the only thing left for me to do was to pray. I fervently asked for God's help. He answered me … me, the man who'd always professed not to believe, was answered by God.

"My next move was to try reaching her on the phone again. This time she answered the phone, saying how she hoped I wasn't too worried. I cannot describe the relief I felt. She'd become lost in the traffic and heavy rain but now was on the right path to the ferry, thanks to a kind couple who had noticed her parked at the side of the road and pulled over to help her. That day prayer and kindness had joined forces.

"I cannot tell you how grateful I was to know she was alright. I thanked God. I thanked Him for answering my prayer. From that day onward, no longer was I a non-believer. Some would say believing is a leap in faith, but I also learned from that particular experience that to go in the opposite direction would be a danger-ous leap … with consequence."

He smiled at me before turning and go-ing back to his seat.

One smiling face after another followed, each with a topic they'd been assigned under the umbrella of Love and Kindness. When the last one had finished speaking, the assembly exited, one after the other with a light shining in their eyes like beacons to pending joy, just as they'd ap-peared when I first saw them. They'd spo-ken with great earnest, delivering words with such expression it sounded like music to my ears. I felt saturated, and although I likened each talk to a church sermon, the saturation I felt seemed to settle in my very core.

Esther stayed back with Sebastian and me, and she pulled a chair up to us.

"Tell me, Jonathan, did you gain some-thing from today's forum? I'm certain you've heard it all before, but did it reinforce what you were taught as a child, or awaken you in any way? Are you able to repeat some of the subjects?" Her voice was gentle.

I was anxious to list the subjects, if for no other reason than to show her I'd been attentive.

"They covered killing and robbing, saying it's at the top of the list, an abomination toward the Creator. They also covered greed, conceit, abusing others, gluttony, which is abuse to one's body, stating body abuse by overeating is not loving oneself. And they covered injustice, disrespect, arrogance, degradation. All of the topics involved love and kindness."

I was proud of myself for being able to itemize so many subjects. I sat thinking about them and how I'd failed in life, but I didn't like to linger there too long. Recognizing my own shortcomings was much too painful for a proud atheist like me.

"And," said Esther, "earlier you learned about envy, prejudice, honesty, and taking care of the Earth. I believe you relived your time on Earth for those subjects and received exoneration for the good deeds you had done."

"Yes, yes I did," I replied, but my thoughts were elsewhere. I pursued them.

"Tell me, if there's a God, why does He allow all of the sorrow and strife on Earth, all of the starving people, all of the wars and the maiming and suffering?"

Esther replied quickly, speaking succinctly with slow deliberation, "God gave man free will, which means we were created with minds with which we independently think, analyze, draw conclusions, and make choices. Men and women have different physical characteristics, but all of humanity is created with the ability and responsibility to manage and have authority over their own lives as well as the rest of physical creation. God gave us a great deal of responsibility, Jonathan, so that through experience we will grow in the ability and strength of character to make the right kinds of decisions. When we chose to obey His commands, God is, in effect, teaching us to think like He thinks. He can't do that by thinking for us. We have the freedom of choice. Eventually, the way we choose to live will have consequences. The consequences will be the result of our decisions.

"On second thought, aren't we glad people aren't more like machines? We wouldn't want to give up our freedom of choice, but it seems like there couldn't be a perfect world unless some higher power had complete control, regulating every aspect of everyone's life. How frustrating would it be to be forced to only eat healthy foods, always go to bed on time, and never skip a daily workout? People would resist. Instead of creating machines or robots, God created people. He gave us free will, the ability to think, reason, and make our own choices.

"He created us with free will for a simple reason: to fulfil His purpose of creating an eternal, spiritual family. He wants His children to choose to be like Him. Does that answer your question, Jonathan?"

"Well, er, er, I don't know. There's a lot to think about."

I was thinking how I'd told myself earlier that I was going to get to the bottom of this—this incomprehensible trip I was on, this out of body, in body, experience, the mysterious stations I'd come to, and the reliving of parts of my life on Earth. I had to get to the bottom of it!

"Esther, I would like you to level with me. Tell me where I am, exactly. I want you to tell me if, in fact, I died and if, in fact, this is all a dream. And who are the people I've met at the stations and all of those people speaking today? Where did they all come from?" I paused and pleaded, "Please tell me!"

"Jonathan, I owe you an apology. I should have told you at the onset. Of course I'll answer your questions. First of all, yes, you passed away. You were killed by a large truck and died very quickly. Thank goodness you didn't have to suffer long."

My thoughts reverted back to the accident, which now seemed like a century ago.

"Right now, Jonathan, you're at the last station for the Rules for Living on Earth. In fact, you're just outside the gates of Heaven, and all of the people you've met along the way are angels of God, the Creator."

I put my hand on my chest, swallowed, and gasped. "Just outside the gates of Heaven? Angels? Are you kidding me? The gates of Heaven! Good grief, I don't believe in God! How can there be gates of Heaven? I died an atheist."

I was quiet for a few seconds as I plunged deep in thought. Finally, I spoke again.

"W-w-what's on the other side? Do I need a password or a key? How do I pass through the gate?"

"Oh, Jonathan, you're so close to finding out. We're a bit ahead of ourselves, though. We have one more subject to cover. As they say, the best is left for last. In this case, it's not only the best, but the most important of all. Can you guess what that is?"

Still in shock, I glanced quickly at Sebastian, who had been faithfully sitting beside me with an expression that remained stoical. Reverting my gaze back to Esther, I scratched my head and shrugged my shoulders.

Esther continued, "It is vitally important, and the lack of it has been the cause of much sadness on Earth. It has caused wars between nations and within families. I'm talking about forgiveness, Jonathan. Many people have never been able to forgive. It stabs at their soul like a thousand knives. To carry an unforgiving heart is like carrying a sack of stones on your back for the rest of your life. Some humans have lost their mind over it, while others have committed murder or suicide. To forgive and to sincerely ask for forgiveness is the supreme act of love and kindness and will bring instant joy."

Esther paused, folded her hands on her lap, and gave me a long look with eyes bright with conviction.

"With all due respect," I said, "there are some things that are unforgivable. For example, a murder in the family, damage of one's home, deprivation of visitation of children when a marriage has broken up, physical and mental abuse. I'm just naming them at random and could go on. There are many unforgivable deeds. I know I could never just forget and forgive, never get over some things."

Esther replied, "When someone apologizes or even when they don't, we must forgive them. The only way we can be set free is to forgive. We cannot expect others to forgive us if we can never forgive anyone else."

"I'm not asking anyone to forgive me. No need."

"Do you think you've led a perfect life on Earth?"

"No, I don't think anyone has. Who needs to forgive me now if I'm dead?"

"At this point, the Creator needs to forgive you."

I was quiet for a long while, trying to make sense of it all. I asked myself, *If there's no Creator, then how did I come to be here? How did I leave my body as I did?"*

I pondered further with my head in my hands, arguing with myself.

There has to be a Creator, a Supreme Being. There just has to be. I've been wrong all along.

I thought of the many others on Earth—intelligent, prominent people like myself—who didn't believe in God. I wasn't alone; there were thousands of atheists, if not millions, living on Earth. Were they all so badly mistaken?

Now I was at the gates of Heaven and not worthy to pass through. The reality of this thought fell full force. My heart was thumping loudly in my chest, and my throat tightened, threatening to choke me. Overcome with sorrow, I hung my head and couldn't stop the flow of warm tears that began to fall on my lap.

Sebastian leaned his head to mine and put his arm tightly around me. Esther patted my glistening hand, wet from the tears that had fallen there.

She handed me a tissue saying, "There, there now, Jonathan, I know how sad you feel."

Suddenly she clapped her hands, making me jump in my chair. Her pitying voice quickly switched to a gleeful tone. My head came up.

"I have good news, Jonathan, very good news! When the people on Earth were lost and couldn't find their way, when they were sinning and didn't know how to live the way the Lord had instructed them through the Ten Commandments, His love for His people was so great that He sent His only son, Jesus, down to Earth to show people the way, and to bring them good news. Jesus spent many days instructing His followers, the apostles. They kept notes when He spoke and then in chronological order wrote down all that He'd taught them. He also gave them a special prayer known as the Lord's Prayer; then they combined all as the New Testament, and added to the book called, the Bible.

"Jesus died on a cross so that your sins could be forgiven, Jonathan. He knew He was going to die, so the night before, at His very last meal, He shared bread and wine with His apostles. He told them when He was gone to repeat it in His memory.

"Many people on Earth read the Bible and many share bread and wine in His memory and say the Lord's Prayer. All you have to do is be truly sorry for your sins and you'll be forgiven. Then you'll be allowed to pass through the gates to Heaven."

"I will?" I asked, choking the words out between sobs and raising my tear-filled eyes. "Will God forgive me? Will He actually forgive me?"

"Yes, He will. That is why, Jonathan, we *must* always forgive others. We must!"

At long last, after a hard struggle within myself, I understood the need for forgiveness, and the messages from all of the other lessons.

"I'm so sorry, Lord!" I declared aloud in a trembling voice that didn't sound like my own.

Suddenly, my heart was lifted and I became excited about the expectation of entering Heaven. A joy well beyond measure totally engulfed me!

Esther led the way. I followed her while Sebastian took up the rear. Silently and slowly, we walked past the circle of empty chairs, across the room, down the long hallway, and through the door marked with the words, Love and Kindness. We moved out onto a path between a grove of yellow rose bushes and, with their scent filling our nostrils, began skipping our way to Heaven.

10

Passing Through

That wondrous scent of yellow roses surrounded us as we skipped along. I could hear a flute playing in the background which, as we drew nearer, changed to piano music. Bach's joyous "Cum Sancto Spiritu," the epic finale to the Gloria, filled the air.

A simply constructed gate made of cedar wood was visible ahead. A sign of similar wood hung overhead with the words edged in black, WELCOME TO HEAVEN. POPULATION: EVERLASTING.

As we drew near, the door swung open and I walked through with my support team of Esther and Sebastian at my side. A voice, loud and soft at the same time, commanded, "COME ON IN, JONATHAN BROWN." It was music to my ears.

"Who was that?" I asked. "He knows my name."

"That was God welcoming you. It will be a while before you meet Him. He's very busy in Heaven; however, you'll see His son, Jesus, soon. He's always strolling about, speaking with people and socializing, especially with the children. In Heaven everybody is friendly. There's no class distinction. All are equal."

I was impressed by Esther's words and I gazed around, astonished at how ordinary everything appeared. I felt it could have been any little town on Earth … or was it a big town, a city perhaps? I had yet to learn. I was expecting to see opulence, a golden gate, and diamonds on the street signs, but instead things were remarkably simple. I wasn't disappointed; somehow ordinary was perfect. As they would say on Earth, no need to be pretentious!

We walked along the quiet street where many people lived in modest little homes. Some were out in their yard tending their flowers, lush and flourishing; many others—men, women, and children—were strolling and passing us on the street. Everyone smiled and greeted us warmly. They all looked extraordinarily happy. I felt they all knew I was the new kid on the block and that I was being given the grand tour.

"You will notice how the avenues and streets have been given special names. We're presently walking on Love and Kindness Avenue," said Esther, a little amused smile on her lips.

I hadn't noticed the sign; I was too busy trying to see everything else. Taking notice, I smiled and took further notice of other signs as we walked past: Compassion, Forgiveness, Generosity, Tolerance, Charity, Modesty, and Contentment, to name a few.

I could see a playground off in the distance where there were a multitude of children frolicking about. In the middle was a young man playing with them. Their laughter sailed through the air like music.

"That's Jesus with the children," said Sebastian, who had been unusually quiet for the past while. "He loves everybody, especially innocent children."

I gazed in His direction, wishing I was closer to get a better look. From what I could see, He looked very much like He'd been depicted in pictures on Earth. There appeared to be an aura of light surrounding Him.

"Tell me, Esther, have all denominations on Earth been allowed in Heaven?

There's such controversy about that subject among people."

We walked along for a few moments before she answered.

"Our Creator has been saddened by that particular discord. We're all God's children. In Heaven there's no discrimination. Every religion, doctrine, faith, belief, as well as non-believers, are given the chance to come home to God." Winking, she exclaimed, "You, for example."

She smiled and continued, "Look across the street at the folks going into that home; they were Muslims on Earth, and a few doors down lives a family that on Earth were Jewish."

"Are there any churches in Heaven? I haven't seen any since we've been walking."

"There's no need for churches in Heaven. Folks here are happy and are exactly where they want to be. They don't have to pray for eternal life, they have it."

"Another question, Esther, if I may. What happens to the people I left behind on Earth? And what about friends and family that already have and will pass away? Will I see them again?"

There was no anxiety in my question, merely curiosity. Angst is non-existent in Heaven.

"People on Earth continue living just as you did before the accident," she replied. "Hopefully they will learn to live as God intended. You'll be happy to know your family, since your death, has joined a church group and are learning about the Creator. And I'll be helping you get in contact with your relatives, in particular your grandparents."

My heart soared at the thought of my family learning about the Creator. It had been my duty as a father to teach my children, and I'd failed so miserably, but now it was happening for them. I was also excited to meet my maternal grandparents, who had been so good to me when I was a child. So many Sundays were spent at their home along with my parents. I loved my Grandma's noodle soup and how she'd always laugh and tussle my hair when we met. My grandfather had been more on the quiet side and kept encouraging me to do well in school. Whenever I'd receive a good mark, I'd always phone him, and I enjoyed the compliments laid upon me. Both of my grandparents had died in a boating accident when they were in their seventies. I recalled how sad I'd felt; it would be a treat to see them now.

However, I was more excited to meet God and His son, Jesus. Anticipation of that was a joyous glow I felt within and all

around myself—very much part of the con-
tented and happy feeling I was experienc-
ing since arriving in Heaven.

Walking farther, we passed a ball diamond where a mixed ball game was in progress. The score board high above the massive crowd read: Saints 3, Converts 6,
bottom of the 9th, 2 away. It looked like
an exciting game. We stopped to watch.

The Saints were up to bat and the bases
were loaded. A small, elderly lady with
a furrowed brow and wearing a nun's habit
came forth from the dugout with a bat. I
was astonished to see Mother Teresa walk
smartly up to the plate. I recognized her
instantly from the many times I'd seen her
on the news.

Her first swing got partially tangled
in the skirt of her habit. The umpire announced in a loud voice, "Strike one."
She wasn't daunted but appeared very determined. She let three more balls go by
and was called on one more strike. Now
she was behind the eight ball. She gazed
around at the loaded bases, prepared her
stance, dusted off her skirt, and clenched
her teeth.

The pitch was a classic strike ball
and she swung with all her might. The
sharp crack echoed throughout that part
of Heaven, soaring the ball out of the

park and winning the game for the Saints. Everyone cheered, most of all Sebastian and me; we were also laughing at the joy of it.

Mother Teresa gently laid down the bat and ran around the bases. The ball went so far amongst the bleachers, she didn't have to run fast. When she touched home base, she humbly walked off back to the dugout.

"She always hit a home run on Earth too," said Sebastian with a chuckle. "That is metaphorically speaking, of course. She was greatly admired on Earth for helping so many poor folks."

I agreed. I had to admit I wasn't surprised to see her in Heaven, but what was more of a surprise is that I should witness her presence and see her play ball.

Time didn't have significance in Heaven. No one was rushing; no one had to. People were just joyfully going about their day. The constant feeling of euphoria gave me time to think back on my life now not with regret so much as gratitude— gratitude that I was in this wonderful place. I cocked my head to hear the sounds of Heaven. I could hear laughter, music in all genres, and the chatter of songbirds. What a delight it all was!

"Are either of you hungry?" asked Esther. "There's a restaurant up ahead."

I'd been so caught up with the sights of Heaven that I hadn't thought about food at all. But now that she mentioned it, I suddenly felt ravenous.

"Does one *have* to eat in Heaven?" I asked.

"There's nothing one *has* to do in Heaven, Jonathan. All of the pleasurable things you experienced on Earth are yours here in Heaven. If you want to experience a great meal, you can just go to a restaurant of your choice and order it."

We walked up the front steps of a home converted into a restaurant. The sign on the outside read: WELCOME TO PALATE PLEASERS.

The eatery was packed with people of all ages enjoying different foods. Some were having sandwiches with salad or french fries, and others were eating full course dinners.

We sat at a round table covered with a white cloth. The centrepiece consisted of a lazy Susan with salt and pepper shakers and paper napkins on top, along with one single daisy in a pencil-slim vase. I remembered the dining experience I'd had with Sebastian when I first arrived at the Love and Kindness station, and what was here paled by comparison. But it didn't matter one iota, such was the relaxed atmosphere in Heaven. I knew from the restaurant's name that I was in for a treat.

The menu was written by hand on a plain piece of paper. I looked it over carefully, astounded at the many choices I had. After several minutes of trying to decide, finally I chose filet mignon with lobster and a vegetable medley for the entrée. For starters, I ordered a shrimp salad and for dessert, cherries jubilee. Esther said she wasn't very hungry, so she ordered a shrimp salad with garlic toast. Sebastian, on the other hand, went for the pasta. He ordered lasagna with meat balls on the top, adding a salad to start.

Bottles of red and white wine were immediately brought to the table by a pretty, young waitress who couldn't stop smiling. She looked liked she was enjoying everything she was doing. Automatically I reached into my pocket for change to tip the waitress.

"No need for that," said Esther. "Money is non-existent here. All is free."

I didn't have a wallet in my pocket, as it were.

We sat and began to enjoy the fantastic meal. Everything was perfect. The lobster dipped in clarified butter was superb. We didn't speak much at the table. We were too much in awe of the great meal we were poised to enjoy.

Suddenly, there was a commotion at the far end of the dining room. Silver cutlery could be heard falling on the tables, along with the scrunching sound of chairs being pushed back.

Jesus had entered the restaurant.

I rose quickly to my feet. I so badly wanted to meet Him. Without hesitation, I walked across the room directly toward Him and extended my hand. As I shook His hand, I noticed the scar was on Jesus' wrist, rather than on His hand—the scar from his barbaric crucifixion. He delivered a firm shake. I didn't know what to say to Jesus. All I could think to stammer was, "C-come and sit with us. Please."

Jesus, wearing a white tunic and pale blue jeans, stood about five-foot-ten, and though He was of medium build, the breadth of His shoulders indicated strength. His olive skin and dark hair and eyes were indicative of His Middle Eastern heritage. A second glance at His large, dark brown eyes gripped the onlooker, for within shone a thousand lights reflecting the epitome of kindness; this coupled with the awesome power to look into one's soul spoke of his divinity.

Jesus nodded and smiled warmly at everyone, patting the top of children's heads as He slowly walked over to the table where Esther and I stood, anxiously waiting. He sat down in the empty chair. It was as though it was meant for Him. And it was.

The tables held a variety of people, each with someone in particular to dine with: grandfathers with families, neighbours with neighbours, young couples with perspective in-laws, mothers with daughters, birthday celebrants joined by their families. All had someone special, none more so than myself and my party. Once seated, a plate of fish and chips was quickly brought to Jesus. He turned to me. "I'm happy you're here," He said, reaching for the tartar sauce. "I know it was a long and hard, tough struggle out of atheism to join my Father and I here in Heaven."

"Yes, my Lord, indeed it was. I'm so happy to be here, but I don't feel worthy … like I shouldn't be here."

Jesus smiled. "You made it through the stations of the Rules for Living on Earth, and although along the way you didn't speak it aloud, we heard you asking for forgiveness long before you did at the end. My Father and I saw the goodness in your heart."

I felt a warm glow from Jesus' loving words, but I still needed to find some answers. I cleared my throat.

"May I ask You some questions, Jesus?"

"Of course you may. I'll be happy to answer any questions you might have." His smile spread warmth around the table.

"Well … there are many anthropologists who claim man and apes have descended from the same ancestor. They hold fast to this premise and teach it in school at all levels. That proclamation has never received an adequate response to the contradiction that God created man."

"There are things on Earth my Father uses as a test to the faith He wants man to have. Creation is one of them. He has allowed a small unravelling of creation to test faith. A similar test involves cosmology technology. Man has questioned whether there is life on other planets beside Earth and are working diligently to discover this. All I can say is that if my Father wants to share other creations, He will do so, and if He does, in no way does one diminish the other. Remember, my Father created the universe and all that is in it."

To my great surprise, I accepted this. I swallowed hard and could actually feel the new light in my eyes. Jesus' answer seemed to uncomplicate the deep-routed studies presented by the highly educated historians.

"Also, Lord, there are many things plaguing Earth. I speak mainly about wars. Will there ever be an end to this horror?"

"In order for things to change on Earth," replied Jesus, "people around the world have to start at the beginning. By that I mean they have to start with the children. As soon as a child can understand, the fundamentals of peace should be taught, such as love, forgiveness, kindness, re-spect, and consideration. It should be ingrained. It's imperative this happens in every family and is part of the cur-riculum in every school. It must be rein-forced daily along the way. Consequently, when the child is grown, his or her peace-ful nature will be so strong, fighting with another would be unthinkable, and nations will be at peace."

I sat quietly pondering over what Jesus had said and was trying to imagine a peaceful world. I tried to imagine how the fundamentals of peace could be taught to children all around the world. It brought me to another question, and I was hopeful there might be a connection.

"Another question I have, Jesus, is something I've not been able to understand.

It's something I've wondered about whenever it was referenced on Earth at funerals and at bank conventions when grace was said before meals. What exactly is meant when there's a reference to the Holy Spirit? I realize Your Father and Yourself and the Holy Spirit are considered to be the Trinity. But what exactly is the Holy Spirit, and what is meant by the Trinity?"

"First of all," Jesus replied, "My Father, the Holy Spirit, and myself are one. We are the Trinity. I know that mysticism is hard for mortals to understand. On Earth, people honoured the Trinity by making the cross a symbol. Recognizing the Trinity is intrinsic to having faith. And similar to kindness, faith should be developed in children; however, when it arrives in adulthood, it's a special gift.

"The Holy Spirit is, as its title indicates, a spirit. The Spirit comes in many forms and has mystical powers. It opens and gladdens the heart, delivers faith, makes one see the light, and showers goodness upon deserving souls. When called upon, it opens the eyes of nonbelievers and gives hope to mankind. Everyone in Heaven has been filled with the Holy Spirit."

"Thank you, Jesus. I'm so honoured to have had it all explained by You and to have received the Holy Spirit." I placed my hand over my chest. "My heart has been gladdened."

Esther and Sebastian both sat very still while Jesus was talking, silently nodding and smiling, first at Jesus, then at me.

"What do you do here in Heaven?" I asked.

"There's something you must realize ... Heaven is very much the same as on Earth but with these exceptions: everyone's happy here, there's no competition, no currency, and no shortage of anything one might need. Literally gas tanks are always full.

"Everyone's busy, and so am I," continued Jesus, "There are people every day arriving from Earth. I try to meet with them just as I'm meeting with you today. And my Father wants me to be available should He need me for a special mission or project, such as the one I'm planning for Him right now."

"Are You able to tell us, Lord?" asked Esther.

"It's a special entertainment project. But first I have to build a stadium, or theatre, so to speak. I'm enlisting all the help I can get. There are many carpenters, plumbers, and electricians here in Heaven."

We sat wide-eyed and spellbound by Jesus' plan.

"I'm hoping you three will help as well. I will need an area search for the best site. Once built, I will need someone to help with the interior design, and finally someone to book and organize the shows."

"What kind of shows?" asked Sebastian.

"Talent shows, for a starter. My Father has given everyone on Earth varied talents that must be shared. Musical talent especially is to bring joy to people, especially to people who are suffering in one way or another and need some cheering. The talent My Father gave can be put into three categories: talent discovered and developed; talent discovered but not developed; and talent not discovered at all. There's much talent here in Heaven, folks who performed on Earth and others who always wanted to perform but just didn't get the opportunity. I happen to know, Jonathan, that you're a great pianist, and your talent didn't get past your own walls. This will be your chance to share your talent. You will also be very good at organizing the construction of the theatre and compiling the show. Being a banker on Earth has given you great organizational skills. If you can organize money on Earth, you can organize people here in Heaven.

"And you, Sebastian, even though you're on the quiet side, I also happen to know you were a great speaker and earned many awards on Earth. You will make a wonderful Master of Ceremonies, and you're good with a hammer too.

"And you, Esther, were renowned for your interior design and decorating. You will be a tremendous help with the construction, best use of interior space, and choice of colours. And I'm sure you will be helpful in the design of the stage settings."

Esther and Sebastian's eyes—and, I assumed, my own—were shining brighter than the morning sun. It was going to be so much fun being involved in this project, especially with the supreme carpenter, Jesus. We were excited about what role we might play in helping bring this amazing idea to fruition.

"When do we start?" asked Sebastian.

"As soon as you can … today if it works for you."

"I think I know of a possible site or two," he replied.

"Wonderful! Can we meet again in two hours, say behind the ball diamond you saw me at earlier today? There's a great little park there where we can sit and discuss this further."

"We'd better finish our meal before it gets too cold," said Johnathan.

Jesus smiled broadly, showing perfect, white teeth, for He knew it was a moot point; in Heaven, food always stays warm.

11

Little Donkey

When the delicious meal concluded and we prepared to take leave, Jesus looked at His watch and said, "It's six o'clock now. You have two hours to drive around Heaven to find a site for our new building. I hope that works for you."

He dug deep into his pocket and drew out a set of keys, which he handed to me. "There's a blue car parked in the lot at the side of the restaurant. You can't miss it; it has an animal painted on the driver's door." He gave us a mischievous wink.

"As soon as you find the site suitable for our new venture, just wait there and I'll join you."

With that, He turned and led the way back through the restaurant, stopping and greeting people who were quick on their feet. A trail of little children followed Him to the door before being summoned back by their parents.

When the three of us reached the door of the restaurant and stepped outside, Jesus was nowhere in sight. We stood scanning the large parking lot for the blue car. We saw several blue cars.

"Let's go have a closer look," said Esther. "We have to look for an animal painted on the door."

Up and down the lot we walked, looking at each and every blue car, but to no avail.

"There's one way over there," I said, pointing toward the farthest corner of the large lot.

I hurried over to it, Esther and Sebastian right on my heels. That blue car had something painted on its door. We broke out into laughter when approaching closer; we saw that it was a little donkey. *Now I know why Jesus winked,* I thought.

"How appropriate!" Esther said with a laugh. "Now let's go find the site. I know of several areas to look at. There are two lots on Happiness Avenue and another at the top of a hill just past Rainbow Street."

We stepped into the car and, with me behind the wheel, drove off.

"You'll have to tell me where to go," I said.

"Turn right up ahead at the lights, then take a sharp left on Happiness Avenue."

We'd driven for several miles when Esther exclaimed, "There it is! That's the first lot I had in mind."

"I think it's too small," remarked Sebastian.

I pulled over to the side of the road. "There wouldn't be enough space for a parking lot," I said.

"Well then, let's look at the second possible site," Esther suggested.

We drove again for several miles before coming to the next site, but it appeared smaller than the first one, so we drove on.

"You have to make a left turn up ahead on Rainbow Street.

I hope the next one will be better than the first two."

We drove up a long, steep hill, coming to a dead end at the top. A large, treed area faced the road. There was a sign that read, "Building Site—Five Acres."

"That's it," said Esther. "I didn't remember it being that large. The sign wasn't there when I saw it last."

"Wow!" exclaimed Sebastian as we exited the vehicle. "I think it's perfect. What do you think, Jonathan?"

"Yes, I think so too. Besides, there will be a nice view down Rainbow Street with all of its flowers."

As I walked, kicking a few loose stones along the way and looking around, I saw a hint of cerulean blue amongst the emerald cedars.

"There's a lake off to the right. Once the building is up, there will be a fantastic view there as well. This is becoming more exciting by the minute."

We agreed this was the spot. No sooner had we come to this conclusion when a crackling in the woods grabbed our full attention. I expressed the thought that perhaps there was a bear in the woods, but to our surprise, Jesus stepped forward.

He smiled.

"I see you've chosen this spot. Actually, I think it's perfect. There's a little café within walking distance from here. Let's go there, have some refreshments, and make plans."

With Jesus leading the way, we strolled down Rainbow Street. The sun was shining on our shoulders and the air was fresh. There were a few businesses interspersed with residences and many flower boxes everywhere displaying a kaleidoscope of colours. We arrived at a quaint little coffee shop. When we entered, a hush descended upon the room. All were happy to have Jesus in their midst. He smiled and raised His hand to prevent them from standing.

We chose a booth at a far corner and ordered a round of coffee and a platter of delicious pastries. Jesus took out a notepad and pen from inside His tunic and handed it to me.

Feeling the pressure of having just been designated as the man in charge, I said, "We'll have to deal with first things first, and these are my suggestions. Number one: hire some loggers to clear away the timber so we can see the lay of the land and the size of the lake; then bring in heavy equipment to clear the trees and whatever stumpage remains."

Esther was quick to speak up. "I think we should engage an architect to give us some designs for the building. I would like to see a conference room, perhaps a dining and dancing area, and finally a great stage for the talent you said is here, Jesus." She turned to see Him smile and nod.

Sebastian, who had worked in construction on Earth while going to university, clearly felt his input would be valuable. He said, "We'll need a general contractor who will engage all of the necessary people, such as plumbers, electricians, and of course a variety of carpenters."

Jesus turned to me. "When you needed to hire staff for your bank on Earth, how did you go about it?"

"There were employment agencies to draw from, and in earlier days, we placed a classified ad in a local paper, but more recently, all of our hiring was done via the Internet."

"It looks like we will be using the Internet," said Jesus.

I'd been taking a few notes on the pad Jesus had given me. I turned first to Esther.

"Would you please find an architect?"

Then I turned to Sebastian and asked him to round up some loggers and excavators.

"The first thing I have to do," I said, "is to find an apartment or house. Right now, I'm homeless."

"I was about to tell you, that's all been looked after," said Jesus. "You've been given an apartment nearby, furnished and equipped with a telephone and computer. The fridge is also well-stocked. Actually, it's quite a large apartment and can substitute as an office and meeting place. The address is 1111 Encore Street. It's the second street off Rainbow. And by the way, the little donkey car is yours, as is this."

He reached into the pocket of His tunic and handed me a cell phone.

"Thank you, Jesus," I replied, "I wasn't expecting any of that."

Jesus stood up. "By the way, there's no need now to meet in the park." With that He smiled and walked out of the coffee shop.

I turned to Sebastian and Esther. "We do need to exchange phone numbers."

We did so quickly.

"Also, when you have people in mind for the positions, arrange for them to be interviewed at my place. We can jointly do the interviewing. Just let me know; I can be ready at a moment's notice.

"But before we depart, I'd especially like to thank you, Sebastian, for helping me up the stairs to Heaven and being my faithful guide and companion."

Sebastian's lazy smile spread slowly across his face. He put out his hand to receive my shake.

Esther said, "I remember when Sebastian first arrived, and although his passage was less strenuous, he showed the same heartfelt gratitude."

I turned to Esther. "There are no words to express how grateful I am to you! Your forum on Love and Kindness and your explanation of Forgiveness brought me to the Lord and to this wonderful place!"

I embraced her and kissed each of her flushed cheeks.

As we drove away, the setting sun cast a yellow glow down Rainbow Street, catching the corner of every building and the lip of every colourful petal, each one more beautiful than the other, yet equal. It gave full credence to its name and flooded the three of us with elation.

12

New Digs

Encore Street consisted of single-residential homes with two small apartment buildings, one next to a children's playground and the other above a convenience store. I'd never been keen on shopping in large grocery outlets and was therefore pleased the address given me was the latter.

I was also pleased with my apartment … a bit overwhelmed was more like it. I categorized it as superb for my existence in Heaven and could not help feeling undeserving.

The foyer held a closet for outerwear and a "welcome" foot mat tucked up to the entrance door. It was positioned on ceramic tiles that carried on into a compact kitchen with gleaming, granite counter tops and stainless steel appliances. I opened the cupboards and was pleased to see solid, white dishes and bowls carefully placed on the shelves, and in the drawers a collection of pots and pans along with cutlery and utensils.

Shining cherrywood floors ran throughout the entire space and into the adjoining dining and living room area, where a beige sofa and chairs invited visitors to be seated. A large, round coffee table sat in this room's centre.

All walls were painted in earth tones that, along with the rich wooden floors, produced a certain warmth to the entire space.

I walked back into the kitchen and opened the door marked "pantry," and there to my delight I saw shelves stocked with staple items such as flour, sugar, coffee, tea, cereals of all kinds, spices, and an indescribable amount of canned goods.

If I thought the pantry was well-stocked, I had yet to open the fridge. When I did, I gasped! All of the food groups were abundantly addressed—milk, butter, cheese, vegetables, meats, and fruit were all lined up in neat order. I realized all the food was not a necessity but merely a pleasure.

Momentarily overwhelmed but not daunted, I made my way back into the living
room and sat down in one of the plush
chairs. I gazed around the room and could
see through into an adjoining room where
there was a large conference table with
a laptop at one end surrounded by twelve
chairs, clearly meant for planning and
hiring—the thought coursed an unexplained
excitement through my body!

My gaze found a small alcove off the
living room, and to my delight there
stood a piano. On closer inspection, I
saw it was a Steinway, and piled high on a
shelf next to it were sheets of music of
all description.

Still overwhelmed, I thought about my
life on Earth and all that had transpired
since my untimely death. I was grateful
those thoughts were now angst-free … thank
Heaven for that. I'd come a great distance, successfully passing through the
different stations and surmounting many
obstacles before finding my Saviour who
had died so sins could be forgiven, died
so I would be allowed to pass through the
gate into Heaven.

As I sat in the comfort of the sofa
chair, my elbow on the arm and resting
my head on my hand, I pondered why I'd
been selected to oversee such an important task. A task God Himself had ordered.

I wondered why I'd been given this special assignment of building a large theatre and conference centre. Surely there were others in Heaven who were more qualified. I decided I would ask Jesus the next time I was in His presence.

Feeling a bit drowsy, I decided to have a nap. The bedroom was as lovely as the rest of the home, and the large bed beckoned for me to lie down. I slipped off my shoes, rolled back the bedspread, and lay down. The bed was firm and the bedding smelled like lilacs, as though recently laundered. I inhaled deeply, and soon I was fast asleep.

I didn't know how long I'd slept. It must have been all night, for now I was totally refreshed, the sun was shining brightly through the windows, and I was mighty hungry. Half an hour later, with the aroma of bacon frying, two eggs on the counter, and a hot cup of coffee in my hand, I set about to make plans for the day.

Having finished my breakfast, I opened the notebook to where I'd logged in Esther and Sebastian's phone numbers. I punched in Esther's number first.

"Good morning, Esther, or is it afternoon? I'd like for us to meet today, say around noon here at my place. There's tons of food in the fridge for our lunch. Are you free to come?"

"Sounds great; I'll be there. By the way, it's 9:30 a.m. I haven't been up that long. See you later; bye."

Next I called Sebastian. His phone rang several times before he answered.

"Hello, you just got me out of the shower," he said, laughing.

"Sorry about that. Can you come here today for a meeting at noon? I'll have lunch on, and we can go over our plans for the big project. Esther will be here too."

"You betcha; I'm looking forward to it. Wow! We sure have a big job ahead! See you at noon."

I checked the pantry for a can of salmon to make sandwiches for my luncheon guests. I had to make a choice between that and tuna and settled on the latter. Mayonnaise and chopped dill pickle turned the contents into a delectable mix. My mother had taught me well. Luckily there was fresh bread. I filled a platter with wrapped sandwiches and placed them in the fridge. Next, a further search in the pantry produced bags of chocolate cookies and cinnamon buns, which I also arranged on a platter.

A pot of tea should complete the lunch, I thought happily. *We mustn't be hungry when we have such big plans to make.*

Esther and Sebastian arrived precisely at twelve noon. Both had attaché cases in hand, smiling and ready for business.

"We'll have our lunch first," I suggested. "I told myself a few moments ago that we mustn't be hungry when making big plans."

After I cleared the table of the empty platters, we settled down to business.

"The first task on the agenda is to get the lot cleared."

Before I could say any more, Sebastian snapped open his briefcase and withdrew a sheaf of papers. Esther smiled.

"I've gathered some companies that we can contact. There are quite a lot of excavators here in Heaven," said Sebastian. "I have ten here." He held up the papers. "I told them we'd contact them today for an interview."

"And I have several architects that we can call," said Esther.

"Wonderful!" I exclaimed, barely able to refrain from clapping my hands. "Grass doesn't grow under your feet. Let's get phoning."

And we did. Calls were made, and for the rest of the day we interviewed several people. After much deliberation, the choices were made. An architect by the name of Jake Weissmuller was hired, along with a company called Acme Site Preparation, owned by Jim Rathy. We discussed the size and location of the site.

Hurrah, the ball is rolling!

I was elated as I recalled the crucial moments of the day.

Weissmuller had stood up at the table and said, "I'll visit the site when the land is being cleared. I want to know the exact location and size of the lake in relation to the rest of the property. It'll be a wonderful feature for the visual aspects of the centre and a strong component for its appeal. It's also essential a number of trees be left standing. I'll be conferring with Jim Rathy of Acme."

Jim Rathy had declared earnestly he would be on site first thing in the morning and that his crew was expected to have the land cleared within two weeks, if not sooner.

I thought about the day's process and all of the people who had streamed through the door to be interviewed. I thought about the two men we'd eventually hired.

I'd sat at many a contract table on Earth as banker/financier where reputability and cost were the deciding factors that made the ink hit the paper. But here, here in Heaven, it was all about availability, workmanship, and timetable. Mere existence here depicted integrity, and a handshake sealed the agreement.

I commented to my colleagues, "Isn't it amazing how quickly contracts can be agreed upon when there's no currency on the line?"

"It sure is," agreed Sebastian. "Things are so much easier in Heaven." His smile was tight to the corners; it couldn't have been bigger.

"Not only easier," said Esther, "but absolutely enjoyable!" Her words brought a new shine to her eyes.

"So much has happened in the short while since we've been in Heaven, there's something I neglected to give you." She reached into a bag by her side and withdrew a thick, white book.

"Here's a list of people who live in Heaven. No doubt you will want to get in touch with some people you knew on Earth—your grandparents, for example. Sebastian and I'll be leaving you now to explore on your own. Just give us a call when you want to visit the site to see how Jim Rathy is doing with the clearing."

"I'll do that," I said. "Thanks for all your help. There's something I need to ask you before you go, something foremost in my thoughts."

I paused and looked earnestly at each in turn, silently contemplating my question for a few moments before speaking.

"When will I meet God the Father?"

"God is always with us. He's everywhere," said Esther, sweeping her arms in a circle. "When He wishes to show Himself to us, He will, but be comforted in knowing He is always with us and always around us. His Spirit bubbles within us." She looked me in the eye and added, "Like effervescence."

"I can't help wondering what He looks like."

"We were taught on Earth that God created man in His own image. The next time you're wondering, that should help your imagination."

13

Mystery Solved

I was left with those sagacious words and felt appeased. When Esther and Sebastian took their leave, I poured myself another cup of coffee and sat down in the living room. The thick white book with HEAVEN'S RESIDENTS engraved in gold on the cover lay on the round table in front of me. I picked it up and held it in my hands for a time, staring in wonderment at the cover before opening it.

Had there been only a few Browns in Heaven, I wouldn't have been stymied in finding my grandparents. I poured through pages and pages, looking for J.T.L. Brown. Three initials made it somewhat easier but didn't diminish the commonality. At last there it loomed, halfway down page 10,302.

A flashback loomed in my mind as I re-called the day they'd both drowned in a boating accident. I was ten and grief-stricken at my loss. With shaking fin-gers, I punched in the number.

"Hello, Gramma." I couldn't remember when I'd spoken to her last on the phone and wondered if I would recognize her voice after all of these years.

"Is that you, Johnny Boy, my grandson? It has to be you, I had only one grand-child. It has to be you!" Her familiar voice was warbling with excitement.

"When did you leave Earth?" Before I could answer, she called to my grand-father, "John, John, come quick! Johnny Boy's in town!"

I didn't hesitate to pay them a visit. Dahlias in softest yellow to a deep ma-genta, interspersed with white daisies, like something one would see in a flower book, flanked each side of the road as my car, with a donkey painted on the door, moved slowly up the long driveway.

Both of my grandparents stood on the veranda of the small white cottage, await-ing my arrival. They were exactly as I re-membered them. I knew they would be sur-prised to see me at my present age and would have to adjust. It didn't seem to be of any concern, though, for they hugged me and declared how happy they were that I'd come.

"You've grown up to look so much like your father," they both declared. "Same dark, curly hair and brown eyes. Even though you were only ten when we left Earth, we'd recognize you anywhere."

The Johnny Boy nickname they'd labelled me with as a child was hardly appropriate for the middle-aged man I'd become.

"Come in, come in," said my grandfather, a man near six feet tall who'd always been a giant in my little boy's eyes. Now, however, I could look him directly in the eye.

"We have tea made and the chocolate cookies we know you always liked so much," said my grandmother, neat and proper in her little, pink apron. She led the way into the cozy habitat before hurrying into the kitchen.

"Thank you," I said loudly enough to reach my grandmother's ears in the kitchen, from where the sound of clanging dishes could be heard as she prepared the tea.

I sat down on the plush sofa across from my grandfather and gazed around the room. It reminded me so much of how their home used to be when I visited as a child—doilies under the lamps, dish of candy on the end table, and a picture of myself playing the piano at a recital.

"Please tell me about our son and your mother, how they are, I mean were, when you left Earth," said my grandfather.

"They're both as well as can be expected for their age. They live in an assisted living home. They like it there; there are always lots of activities planned for them, and they actively participate."

Looking pleased, my grandfather stated, "It's a good thing we don't feel sorrow or loss in Heaven, because as you probably already know, there's no grief or anxiousness here. Did you leave behind a family?"

"Yes, a wife and twin sons, both in college."

My grandmother returned with the tea and cookies and placed them on the coffee table next to the posy of dahlias. She'd always been very much a flower person, as I recalled.

"Do you take cream and sugar?" she asked in her familiar gentle voice.

"Yes, thank you, Gramma."

"Have some cookies; there's plenty back in the kitchen. We are a little surprised to see you here. Your father didn't teach you about the Lord when you were growing up. How are your sons … I mean, I hope your sons will know Him."

"Sad to say, I didn't give my boys a good example. I was an atheist all my life. After I was killed in a road accident, I came slowly through the Rules for Living on Earth. It was a long and arduous journey because I found it very difficult to leave atheism behind. I was lucky to find the Lord just outside the gates of Heaven. The Holy Spirit came within me and filled me with joy." Then remembering what Esther had said, I added, "Like effervescence.

"I'm so happy and ever so grateful! I've also learned my sons and wife on Earth started attending church, so there's hope for them, and that makes me even happier."

Questions came one after the other. I was anxious to answer them all and had a question of my own as well.

"Do you still play the piano? You were a great pianist at a very young age," asked my grandfather.

"Yes, I do. I find it very cathartic. I mean, it helps me to relax. There was a wonderful Steinway waiting for me here in Heaven."

"Tell us about your wife," asked my grandmother. "Where did you meet and what did you do together as a family?"

This was a tough question for me to answer. It was hard for me to remember what we'd done collectively. I'd been away so much with banking and other secret business, although my conscious had been cleared, the latter, my mistress, wasn't anything I was proud of or wanted to recall and relate, especially to my grandparents.

"My wife was a loans officer in the bank I worked at, a beautiful girl and a great wife and mother. My boys and I spent quite a lot of time in the marsh checking out the water fowl. We were keenly interested in the Virginia rail."

"What education did you receive and what kind of work did you do on Earth?"

"I attended the University of British Columbia where, as you know, my father was a professor. I studied accounting and finance. I acquired a Master's degree and a Doctorate of Business Administration. My job took me to various cities around the world, hosting seminars. I sat in boardrooms of large corporations, helping them plan their budgets, and with new companies planning the capital needed at their start up—this, of course, all under the umbrella of my bank affiliation. I loved my work, and I was very successful."

"We're very proud of you, Jonathan!"

"Thank you," I replied. It was the first time I'd heard either of them call me Jonathan … a very pleasant sound indeed!

I used the pause in their questioning to ask one of my own. "Please tell me how your boating accident happened. Everyone wondered about that. I was so sad when you both died. Life just wasn't the same."

"It was the damnedest thing," said Granddad. "We'd gone out early that day in our row boat to do a little fishing. You remember the boat, we took you out in it often when you were a lad. I remember it was one of those most gorgeous of days— big blue sky, bright sunlight. We'd been trolling for awhile when all of sudden, I got the biggest bite of my life that pulled the boat along. I just wasn't going to let it get away. I hollered to your gramma to come and help, that I didn't think I could hang on. She came to my rescue and grabbed onto the rod with me. This, however, put the boat out of balance and it tipped over. We were pulled under quickly by that whopper of a fish! It dragged us lower and lower into the water. Why we didn't let go of the rod, I'll never know. We ran out of breath before we could make it back up to the top. Death was easy. I'd always said, I hoped we'd die together. He smiled, as did his wife.

I smiled too. "Well, I must say, it's wonderful to be with you now. We can visit back and forth," I said.

"How will you be passing your time here, Jonathan?" asked my grandfather. "Every once in a while, an assignment comes to us from the Lord. We've helped out with the Rules for Living on Earth and have buddied up with new arrivals. All is very enjoyable."

"I've been given an exciting assignment," I replied. "I'm to supervise a large entertainment centre that's being built on five acres at the end of Rainbow Street. I'm told this will give people a chance to share their talents with the residents of Heaven."

"That's amazing! We certainly will look forward to attending the shows," said Gramma, beaming. "I know many people will appreciate having the opportunity to see them. Maybe you can play the piano. It was a shame you didn't do that on Earth."

My grandfather added, "And to think you'll be master-minding this endeavour is surely a compliment." A slow smile crept across his face and dimpled his cheek, one I remembered so well when Granddad was pleased about something.

"Once again, Jonathan, we're very proud of you!" said my grandmother.

"Thanks. I must be on my way. I have some calls to make when I get back to my home on Encore Street. A street appropriately named, don't you think? Here's my phone number." I handed her a piece of paper with my cell phone number on it.

"I can't tell you how happy I am to see you both after all these years! Let's stay in touch often. As soon as the building starts to go up, I'll take you there so you can see the progress, I promise."

I hugged both of them at the same time then drove back home in my little donkey car.

14

Progress

A few days later, Esther, Sebastian, the architect, Jake Weismuller, and his general contractor, Gordon Conway, and I planned to meet on site. As I drove up Rainbow Street, I was met by several trucks coming in the opposite direction. Some were loaded with logs and others stumpage with great clumps of earth hanging onto the roots.

When I arrived at the site, I was amazed at the progress already made. Now it was possible to see the lake on the adjacent lot, leaving ample room for the large building and a parking lot. They were waiting for me when I parked the car and walked over to where they were standing.

"Good morning," I said. "Wow! I didn't think there would be this much progress in so short a while!"

"I'm impressed too," said Jake Weismuller. "I'm really pleased the lake is on the property at the right. It gives us more area for a substantial parking lot at the back."

Both Esther and Sebastian stood by, gazing out over the land.

"Sure looks different once cleared," I said.

"I'm anxious to see what kind of building we're constructing," said Esther.

"Well, I can give you a bit of a look at it. I have a rough drawing with me," stated Jake Weismuller. He spread a drawing across the hood of his car to show us the rough, initial drawing.

"This is just a rough illustration. We all have to take a close look at it. Then with your input and I'm sure a few drafts, we'll do the final. I'm anxious to get there so construction can begin. Fortunately, we don't have any city regulations to concern ourselves with. Heaven is a dream for contractors.

"You can see there are three floors. The first one is the recreation area, for activities such as badminton, bowling, and swimming. The second floor will be the theatre where we'll have our talent shows, live theatre, and musicals. The top floor is divided into two parts; one half is a restaurant and dancing area with a sweeping view across Heaven and, of course, the lake.

"The second part of the top floor will be the caretaker's residence. He'll be in charge of maintenance of the entire building and will, of course, hire people to do the job."

"I think it looks great," I said. "I especially like the fact that there will be a view of the lake. I can also visualize great landscaping to complement the building."

Jesus will be so pleased at this progress, I added to myself.

"It's going to be a dream to decorate the interior!" said Esther with a wide smile.

"When can you be available to go over the interior space?" asked Jake.

"Any time; just give me a call."

Sebastian, standing quietly alongside, had, true to form, remained quiet. I could see from his shining eyes that he was clearly relishing his thoughts about being Master of Ceremonies.

"I'll have the final plans ready in about three days," said Jake. "And I'll be engaging a contractor. I have several in mind, some of whom I knew on Earth."

"If that's the case, let's all meet at my place on Friday," I suggested, delighted with the progress that had been made. "Come at noon; I'll fix lunch."

I enjoyed preparing food for others. If there was one positive thing about having no siblings to play with, it was spending countless hours with my mother in the kitchen, watching her every move preparing food … that was, when I wasn't playing piano.

On Friday morning I visited the market and picked out the food I needed. I'd decided on preparing chicken cordon bleu with roasted baby potatoes, green beans almondine, and cherry pie à la mode for dessert. It seemed strange but wonderful to take the food out the door of the store without having to pay for it. I hadn't quite gotten used to there being no currency in Heaven; everything was free and available for all.

My guests arrived as planned, sniffing deeply at the aroma as they walked in. They commented on how impressed they were with the lovely lunch, which was more like a dinner, and we all ate heartily. At the conclusion and when the dishes were cleared and stacked in the dishwasher with the help of Esther, totally sated, we moved into the living room with our cups of coffee.

"Let's talk about a timetable," I said, directing my question to Jake Weismuller and Gordon Conway. "How soon do you think the walls will be going up?"

"Now that the final plans have been completed …" He paused and smiled at Esther to acknowledge her valuable contribution. "I'm told by the contractor the excavator is having the basement dug tomorrow; this will be followed by configuring the services and then the pouring of concrete for the footings."

We spoke at length of the different construction aspects of the large, three-storey building.

"We definitely are making great progress," I commented. "The Lord will be pleased. I was thinking, however, that we should put a sign up, a large one telling everyone what's being constructed. And we should think of a name for our new centre. Let's meet again on Wednesday here at 10:00 a.m. I want each of you to bring three suggestions for a name and then we can select the one we consider the best by general consensus. What do you think? That will give us twelve names to choose from."

There was new purpose on all of our minds when we disbanded, each of us wondering what the other would come up with for a name. One thing we knew for certain: each would give it considerable thought. Wednesday would be interesting, indeed.

And it was!

I placed a dish on the coffee table in which we were to place our suggestions, written on folded pieces of paper. Until we made our final selection, no one would know who had made it. I held a small blackboard on which to write the name as each of us took turns drawing from the dish.

Amid a few *ahahs*, guffaws, and some snickers, the list of twelve names was written. Now the decision had to be made.

We discussed each name. The first to be read was: Heaven's Play House.

Comments were as follows:

"We also have sporting events. I think that should be included in the name."

"We don't have to say 'Heaven;' that's connotative of competition. Besides, everyone knows it's Heaven's."

The next suggestions read were: Happy Haven Entertainment Centre; Happy House; Joytacular; Incredible Castle; Playful House Kingdom; Play House Galore; Ultimate Entertainment; Happy Happenings Hall;

Joytastic; The Genesis; Adventurdo; Boundless Palace; and Second Chance Theatre.

"We have so many suggestions, why don't we throw it out to the public to name?" I suggested. "That will simplify things We can put up a poster with our suggestions on it and a box for new suggestions in the main restaurants."

Once again the results, after three days, were amazing. While there were some new ones, the public unanimously settled on the name Second Chance Theatre. There was little further discussion, as it unanimously hit the nail right on the head. After all, wasn't this what the theatre was all about—giving a second chance to someone's God-given talent that didn't have a chance on earth? Sebastian offered to have a large sign erected over the front door of the building.

COMING SOON
SECOND CHANCE THEATRE

WHERE YOU WILL ENJOY ALL FORMS OF MUSIC, LIVE THEATRE, SPORTING EVENTS, DINING, AND DANCING. ALL WITH A VIEW OF LAKE RAINBOW. For further information, call: Jonathan Brown @ 999-9090.

The task of having the sign put up was given to Sebastian.

And so, two days later, the sign was posted at one side of the lot, well out of the way of the concrete trucks that were moving in and out. The word flew around Heaven faster than an eagle diving for a fish. Day and night excited crowds gathered to check the progress of the massive building being erected.

I left my home on Encore Street, having decided I would take a stroll over to the site. As I walked slowly along I admired the many homes I saw along the way, their pretty flowers in window boxes and alongside their cobblestone walkways. As I passed by, I nodded and smiled at strangers I encountered; their reciprocation was instant.

I thought about this marvellous place called Heaven, where there was nothing but joy in my heart and where life was nothing but one big, happy, and exhilarating existence. If only people on Earth could know how great it was to be here … if only!

I also thought about being filled with the Holy Spirit. And I thought about how pleasurable it had been meeting Jesus and how He'd given me the honour and excitement of overseeing the construction of Heaven's Second Chance Theatre, all for the glory of God.

Yes, life was surely wonderful in Heaven. I realized I'd experienced two thirds of

God. The expectation of meeting the last third, God the Father, face to face hung like a golden cloud in my sky of anticipation. The wonderment of it gave me further joy each night before I fell asleep and each morning when I awoke.

When I reached the project site, I had to work my way through the crowds to get to the edge of the property. The gigantic sign Sebastian had erected in vivid red lettering on a white background stood tall at the corner of the property for all to see … at least all who lived on Rainbow Street. Mounds of black earth surrounded the large, deep hole where concrete had been poured and spread evenly across the five-acre lot. Evidently progress was right on time. Soon lumber and piping would be delivered, and the semblance of the large building would take form. I thought about my promise to take my grandparents to see it once the walls were erected. No doubt this would occur next week.

I was turning to leave when suddenly I felt a gentle pat on my shoulder. It was Jesus! My astonishment quickly left when He spoke.

"Great job, Jonathan!" Then, as quickly as He'd arrived, He was gone.

15

One Hundred Men

Esther awakened with a plan to have a social dinner at her place. After all, Jonathan had had them over several times, so she should be taking her turn. Besides, Jonathan hadn't seen her home.

She picked up the phone and called him first, then Sebastian, then Weismuller, and lastly, Gordon Conway. Jonathan had suggested they discuss the inner workings of the centre, size of the pool, the tennis and badminton courts, and the stage. They all had expressed their delight and agreed to arrive at six for dinner. Now she could plan the dinner and the evening. She decided she would prepare her favourite meal her Earth mother had made: chicken stew with dumplings, homemade buns, and caramel pudding topped with vanilla ice cream. All foods of comfort despite none being needed.

After mopping up their plates and complimenting the cook, they retired to the living room on the top floor of a three-storey apartment building. They complimented her spacious apartment which was not only decorated in lively colours, but also contained a number of tall, green plants that formed a background for her lovely turn-of-the-century furniture. She poured them all steaming cups of coffee and they settled down to their business at hand and extended discussion.

"I would like to thank you, Esther, for inviting us to your attractive residence," said Jonathan, taking the lead. "I know I also speak for the others when I say, once again, we enjoyed a most scrumptious dinner and this equally wonderful ambiance!" He raised his hand in an arc.

"You're welcome," replied Esther, beaming.

"Let's talk about our progress so far and our hopes for the use of the building," continued Jonathan. He turned to Jake Weismuller and Gordon Conway. "Can you give us an update on construction and some idea of completion date?"

"The walls are going up this week, followed by the trusses soon after," said

Gordon. "There's no shortage of carpenters here in Heaven."

"Everything is right on schedule," said Jake. "I'm also calling in a geotechnical company to test the soil and possible requirement of stabilization of soils during construction in case of high ground water levels. I understand sometimes there can be a problem when building near a lake. Although walking over the grounds I couldn't see signs of any additional moisture, I think it's prudent I call them."

Gordon Conway nodded his concurrence.

"Speaking of water," said Esther, "I would like to see a water feature in the middle of the lobby, directly under an atrium where the light can shine on it and create a rainbow. Just think how wonderful it would be to have something signifying the name of the building visible at all times!"

All agreed it was most fitting.

Jake said, "I'll modify the drawings to incorporate this."

"By the way, Sebastian," said Jonathan, "The sign you had erected is magnificent!"

"Thanks. I had worried it may be too tall."

"Not in the least; it's perfect."

"You can see it from that window,"
pointed out Esther. They all moved to the
window. She pointed to the west where the
sign could be seen; albeit just a white
square too far to read, it commanded attention like a beacon. The group felt
proud it was there. They knew the Lord
would be pleased.

"How soon will the building be finished?" asked Jonathan. "I want to know
when to start the staffing of the interior. We'll need clerks for the lobby,
people to take care of the pool, someone
in charge of the café, a sportsman to
be in charge of the badminton and tennis
courts, someone in charge of the dancing
and dining, etc. And most importantly,
the caretaker, who in turn will hire janitors. I'm sure quite a few people will be
delighted to work at the new centre."

Gordon replied, "The walls will up in a
couple of days, and once that's completed, it will go fast. I have many men hired
to work on it." He turned to Sebastian. "I
understand you would like to help as well.
Just come to the site tomorrow morning at
7:00 a.m."

Sebastian grinned, stretching his cheeks
to the maximum. "Yes, sir, I'll be there."

"I'd say within the month we should be
able to start the landscaping. It goes

quickly when there are a great number of men on the job."

"Sounds wonderful!" said Jonathan. "Let's meet again in two weeks for an update. By then, Esther, you should have your interior colours all picked out and whatever else interior decor is required. Plus the landscape drawing should be finished." He looked at Jake, who nodded.

Before taking their leave, they agreed to come together again at Jonathan's home in fourteen days.

* * *

Driving back to my home, I felt elated. I couldn't decide if it was because of the delicious dinner or the amicable company, or perhaps a combination of both.

Soon the magnificent building would be erected, the grounds landscaped, and there standing proud would be the Second Chance Theatre looking very much like it had always been. I could also visualize the parking lot filled with cars whose owners would be enjoying the new premises. And, of course, parked near the front in a special spot would be a blue car—the one with a little donkey painted on the door.

I couldn't help thinking, *Life in Heaven is soooo good!*

16

Construction

"Wow! That's a whopper of a build-ing!" my grandfather exclaimed. "When you said you were supervising the construction of an entertainment centre, I didn't expect it to be so large, son."

We stood at the end of Rainbow Street, my grandparents and I, gazing at the half-constructed building. It stood in the cen-tre of the lot with the blue lake spar-kling from the right. The walls had been erected and the trusses were in place. The many carpenters hammered a tune, filling in the open spaces while others handed them the lumber. It was a sight to behold.

There's something special about a work in progress, I thought. *And special in-deed to have my grandparents here to see it.* I recalled the many days on Earth when

I'd stayed with them and when we'd visited back and forth. They'd made me feel
special and always encouraged me with my
school work and piano playing.

"You and Gramma will be able to come
here to swim, have a nice dinner, and then
spend the rest of the evening dancing. And
not only that, there will be musical shows
to attend as while."

"I can hardly wait!" said Gramma, smiling up at me, her only grandchild. She
couldn't have looked prouder.

"When we have our grand opening, I
want you both to be my special guests," I
told her.

I proudly stood with both hands in my
pockets and a smile on my face. I felt
like I was doing something special for
the two people who had been so good to
me while I was growing up. My grandmother
gave me a hug and kiss on my cheek, while
my grandfather shook my hand.

The day's end came too quickly. We spent
our time together driving around Heaven
and dining in a quaint little restaurant
at the edge of town. We spoke of old times
and relived many pleasant memories.

We also expressed how blessed we felt
to be in Heaven and the joy we felt knowing our Saviour. I took them back to their

cottage, knowing we were all filled with love for one another.

For some reason not even I could explain, I hadn't discussed God the Father with them, or how excited I was at the possibility of meeting Him.

Before two weeks passed, I received the much-awaited call from Jake.

"I didn't think I'd be calling you so soon. I have some good news. All the walls are up now and the roof is on. Progress has been swift. I have up to one hundred men working on it, with the accomplished carpenters directing the others. It's an absolute joy to watch."

I'd been about to call the architect myself and was happy to hear from him.

"That's great! I must go down today to look at it. Do you mean it's now in what is called the lock-up stage?"

Jake laughed. It was the first time I'd heard his laughter. It was melodious, a sound that virtually rippled. "There's no such thing here in Heaven!" He lowered his voice when he said, "No."

"Of course, you're right. There are still some things I need to get used to in Heaven, such as how there are no thieves. And as a banker on Earth, it seems so strange to be living where there's no currency and everything is virtually free. Such privilege we have here! Come to think of it, I guess I don't have to lock my car either, as I've been doing."

This time it was my turn to laugh.

After I hung up my phone, I decided to call Esther and Sebastian, have them over for coffee and doughnuts, and give them the good news. I also had something I wanted to discuss with them.

As happened so often these days, my thoughts turned to God the Father. I hoped God would be pleased, that the new centre would be exactly what He wanted for the residents. And there again was the lingering question: When would I meet Him? The golden cloud of anticipation was shining brighter than ever.

17

The Song

Sebastian paced through his home for several minutes, whistling the tune in his head before picking up the guitar. He sat down on his sofa and strummed the C, G, and F chords for a few moments. His idea of a song for the new centre had dominated his thoughts for many days now. He was waiting for the opportune time to share it with Jonathan, hoping he would find it suitable. Sebastian was meeting with him at a nearby restaurant for lunch today and thought, *I'll tell him then.*

The restaurant, called Munchies, offered a wide variety of luncheon specials. Both Sebastian and Jonathan had expressed a desire for something from the sea, so they ordered clam chowder and shrimp sandwiches.

"Sure looks good," said Jonathan before taking a spoonful of the soup. "I've always preferred Boston over Manhattan when it comes to chowder. Wow, this is delicious!" He picked up the sandwich and took a healthy bite. "This is great too!"

Sebastian concurred, taking a large bite of his shrimp sandwich, then reaching for his napkin and wiping the drip off his chin. After they'd polished off their lunches, they ordered coffee.

"I have something I'd like to run past you," said Sebastian.

"Shoot."

"I think it would be a good idea to have a song, a special song, for the opening of the centre … something that perhaps would stay, something like an anthem. Something that would give the Creator and Heaven what is deserved."

"It's a good idea, but we haven't much time before the opening. We'll have to advertise for a musician who could compose and write the music," stated Jonathan.

"I know someone," said Sebastian, tongue in cheek.

"You do? That would make it more doable. When can we meet with that person?"

"You are right now." Sebastian's laughter filled the room.

Jonathan's jaw dropped. "I didn't know you were a musician. That's wonderful! How soon can you have something put together?"

"I can strum the old guitar and have a rough draft ready in about three days."

Sebastian was beaming. He was looking forward to composing something and writing the lyrics. He knew he could come up with something suitable and felt an inner excitement, which found its way into the large smile he was wearing. A thought flashed into his mind.

"A thought just occurred to me. I think it would be a good idea if you and Esther would contribute a verse or two. I'll be writing one and have already started on the chorus. I think it's important to have all inputs … all of the initial committee of the centre, the founding fathers so to speak." He winked and rubbed his hands together in emphasis.

Jonathan scratched his head. "I just don't know how I would accomplish that. I'm more for hitting the ivories with all the music and lyrics right in front of me, but I'll give it a shot."

***

Later that day when we met with Esther and presented the idea, she was delighted. Instantly she said she would try and write a verse about love, recalling how Jesus had said the greatest of all things is love. Her exuberance was appreciated by Sebastian, and it spurred me into thinking what I would write about.

I thought about my long struggle, the long, exhausting walk I'd taken and the stations I'd weathered my way through, and I thought about how I'd hung onto my atheism right to the bitter end, right outside the gates of Heaven before it all became clear. On Earth I would have been called a hard nut to crack. I smiled at the thought. But most of all it was the Lord's ultimate forgiveness that had grabbed me. I recalled how my heart had leaped when I heard the Lord's welcoming words before I passed through the gate.

I'll write a verse about forgiveness, I thought. *Of course, yes, I'll write a verse about forgiveness.*

Esther poured us a coffee as we sat at her kitchen table. As usual, I took the lead.

"Our centre is nearing completion. The interior walls are up, the painters are coming tomorrow, and in a couple of days the carpet and tile layers will begin their work. We need to think about staffing the centre. Esther, can you look after hiring office staff and a general manager? He or she will know what will be needed staff-wise regarding maintenance, stage management, pit orchestra, etc."

"I can do that," said Esther as she pulled a notepad out of her purse.

"Sebastian, you and I will need to work on the opening ceremony. All three of us need to brainstorm how we'll conduct it. Any ideas?"

"Rather than having just an opening ceremony, let's have a combination, a ceremony and a real show," suggested Sebastian.

"That will mean lining up the talent, giving people a chance to get their act ready."

"And advertising for it."

"What kind of a time line are we looking at?"

"I think two to three weeks should be enough."

"Remember, I have to get the staff in place," Esther reminded us.

I stood up and, resting both hands on the table, spoke. "We don't have to set the exact date today. Let's do the hiring and the advertising, and when we see it coming together, set the date. I think it all depends on how soon we accomplish that."

Esther and Sebastian nodded in agreement and we decided to meet again in a week. Despite the excitement of the completion of the centre nearing an end, it was the verse we had to write that lay uppermost in our minds.

18

Recruitment

A large sign was placed at the end of Rainbow Street and three other specific locations in Heaven. It read:

TALENT WANTED

Calling all singers, poets, acrobats, dancers, musicians, and comedians. If you have always wanted to perform on stage, here is your chance. If you have performed in the past, here is your chance to once again share your God-given talent.

The talent show will be held in conjunction with the opening of our new Entertainment Centre that has been constructed at the end of Rainbow

Street. Coaches will be provided for each category. The date of the opening has yet to be established.

If you would like to participate in any category, please call 250-758-0121.

Response to the sign was overwhelming. My phone never stopped ringing. I kept the conversations to a minimum, just taking down names and phone numbers and promising to get back to them in a few days. To give me a break, Sebastian took over answering the phone. We took down over one hundred names and finally had to leave a message on the phone:

"Please leave your name and number for future shows. We presently have enough talent for the opening."

In the meantime, Esther was in a hiring fever. She first engaged a musical director and production manager. They collaborated on the staff needed, such as stage managers and specialists in lighting, props, and wardrobe. She also hired an office manager and several clerks and, lastly, a building manager who in turn hired several janitors. Most had had theatre experience on Earth.

While this was in progress, all three of us lay in bed at night, trying to compose our verses for the anthem we'd discussed. We'd agreed to meet in a week to present our verses.

It was a bright, sunny day, as most days were in Heaven, when we met in the park just at the corner of Rainbow and Forgiveness Avenue. I sat on a bench with a paper in my hand, and my guitar lying across my knees. Sebastian sat down beside me and took a crumpled piece of paper out of his pocket. We hardly spoke while waiting for Esther. She finally arrived, beaming with joy. She sat and opened her purse and took out a neatly folded piece of paper. We looked at each other in anticipation and a good measure of excitement, wondering what each other had written. Sebastian, who had masterminded the idea, spoke first.

"I've come up with what I think might work as the chorus, and I've also written a verse on talent. He picked up his guitar and began strumming. The chorus went like this:

> Heaven is where I want to be
> Thank you Lord for everything
> For all you've done for me.
> Heaven is where I want to be

"You will note I set the location and have given thanks. What do you think of it?" Sebastian asked us.

"I don't think we could improve it. Great job, Sebastian," I said, meaning every word.

Smiling, Esther nodded in agreement.

I continued, "I wrote a verse on forgiveness, and I think you both will agree it should be the first verse of the anthem. My reasoning for that is because I was forgiven for being a nonbeliever and a sinner on Earth and was welcomed into Heaven when I repented and acknowledged God sent his son to Earth to pay the ultimate sacrifice so all sins could be forgiven."

Both Sebastian and Esther agreed it should be the first verse of "Heaven's Anthem."

"Great! I gave much thought to this and had hoped you'd like it."

Each of us read our verses and made some adjustments. We decided to add a common last two lines on each verse. We were happy with the end results. Sebastian agreed to take the verses and chorus and add the music that had been running around in his head. He picked out the melody on his guitar and hummed. We clapped in appreciation. Then Esther took their papers from us with verses of forgiveness, talent, and love, and read "Heaven's Anthem" aloud in a clear, melodious voice.

"We have our anthem! This is wonderful!" I declared.

I continued, "As you know, we have one hundred people vying for the stage. Auditions will be held in a few days."

"I've hired all the necessary people for the centre, with the exception of the groundskeeper, which I'm presently working on," stated Esther.

We gave each other the high five and laughed aloud!

I'd left my car at home and walked to the park to meet my partners, and now exhilarated from the progress we'd made, I enjoyed strolling back. Chirping songs from the birds flitting through the azure-blue sky filled the air like a small orchestra. It was music to my ears. I passed lovely gardens and neat homes and some restaurants. The many people I passed on the sidewalk smiled and nodded at me. One man who walked past me looked so remarkably like myself that I did a double take. I turned quickly but not quickly enough; the man was lost in the crowd. *Do I have a twin here in Heaven?* I thought rather frantically. *Did my mother give birth to a twin who didn't survive?* I wondered and hoped I would see him again, and should I be afforded the opportunity, I promised myself that I would definitely stop him.

I was looking forward to our agreed meeting at the Second Chance Theatre in two days. The last touches, such as the furnishing, decor, and landscaping, were to be completed today. The very thought that now we could see the results of our efforts made me feel heady.

I recalled how money played such a big role in dictating life on Earth and how it had destroyed so many lives. I thought about my work at the bank and how the interest rate fluctuated every time the world market for, whatever reason, changed. Oh, how different everything was in Heaven, where currency was nonexistent!

The Second Chance Theatre, set amidst tall pines with a brilliant blue lake at its right side, stood like a grand castle in a forest. Pristine lawns encircled the building, and in front, beautiful blue and white heather flanked the sidewalk. In the centre of the lawn to the left and to the right a white marble fountain spurted water high into the air, making a whimsical gurgling sound. The base of the fountains, encircled with mauve, blue, and white petunias, provided perfect contrast.

We'd parked our cars in the parking lot and walked toward the front of the building. The name, Second Chance Theatre, flashed in neon lights above the front door. It beckoned to us to enter. All three of us exchanged glances and gasped through our smiles. What a thrill it was for us to see all of our plans come to fruition!

Entering through the large, double, ten-foot-tall doors, we found ourselves in an entrance fit for a king. Once again there was a fountain, this time in the centre of an atrium. Light shining down on the rising water created a stunning rainbow!

Next to catch one's eye was the cream-coloured walls and marble floor that stretched across the expanse of the vestibule. To the right was a long counter with a granite top with file cabinets behind … obviously the box office and reception area.

We walked past and visited several rooms—a large green room, the backstage area, and finally we entered the area of the stage. It was magnificent! Lights were lined up at the base of the stage, and immediately below, in front, was the pit for the orchestra. Cushioned, graduated seats numbering over two hundred rose like a pyramid across from the stage. A glance upward at the rear of the theatre revealed an opening where the lighting operator would be housed and performing his magic. Both right and left were displayed two rows of balcony seating. Above, the high ceiling had been acoustically constructed for best effect.

"Won't this be so wonderful when the theatre is full and people are performing? I can hardly wait!" said Esther.

"Yes, and the performers will have the thrill of sharing their talent," said Sebastian. "And everyone will be learning "Heaven's Anthem." By the way, Jonathan, we expect you will be playing the piano."

This took me by surprise. "I'd better practice something!"

I was about to speak again to Sebastian when I felt a nudge on my shoulder. Turning, I looked into the smiling face of Jesus.

"Well done! Very well done! My Father is pleased!"

I felt so exhilarated and filled with bliss, I could hardly speak!

"I'm very happy to hear that!" I murmured.

I was preparing myself to say something more to Jesus, but I was hesitant, for the words I was about to speak seemed so inadequate, I wasn't sure how to form them. A few seconds passed before I uttered, "Thank You, my Lord, thank You. I would not be here in Heaven were it not for

You! You made my forgiveness possible. You made this wonderful place of Heaven possible for me to enter! You gave Your life for mankind! Thank You!"

I felt the warmth of His smile.

"You are most welcome, Jonathan. My Father sent me to Earth to bring hope to the people by allowing the forgiveness for their sins. My becoming Man and dying was the impact that carried the strength for them to believe. Like you once did, many struggle with believing. Reading the Bible and hearing God's Word gives them strength and opens their heart.

He turned and smiled at Esther and Sebastian to include them in the conversation.

"You have coordinated the construction of this Second Chance Theatre beautifully. All three of you have worked hard. It's a great venue for the display of talent and will bring joy to many."

Before anyone could say anything further, He walked through the theatre and out the front door.

Later at home, I poured over the stack of music on the small table next to the piano that had been furnished for me. It seemed like years since my fingers had hit the keyboard. In a few moments, however, I

was back in the groove. I played several
pieces, but none seemed to fit the bill.
I worked my way through to the bottom of
the pile, then finally I had the one that
was, in my estimation, perfect in every
way for the occasion!

19

The Show

Rehearsals began the next morning. The production manager and musical director worked diligently with each act; some needed intensive coaching, yet many did not. By the time twenty acts were finalized and combined with the introductions and musical interludes, it was determined the show would run for approximately two hours. I met with them and they told me there was enough talent in reserve to keep the theatre running once a week indefinitely. I was pleased to know that everyone interested in performing would eventually have a chance to do so.

Opening night was scheduled for the following Saturday, with curtain time of 8:00 PM. There was a hum of excitement around Heaven. People were asking each other on the street if they were going to the show.

The tickets were picked up quickly, and those who were too late to get a ticket were comforted with the knowledge that there would be a show every week. Many picked up a ticket for a future show.

***

Bright sunlight splashing through the window on Esther's face awakening her. She sat up in bed, stretched, and instantly thought about the day ahead. She felt excited. After all of the meetings, planning, and hiring, tonight was the grand opening of the Second Chance Theatre. Something else made her excited too. Tonight, she was going to give Jonathan and Sebastian a big surprise!

She'd engaged the talents of an Earth famous artist to paint an image of the theatre. She'd requested the painting be five feet tall by six feet wide, the exact size needed to fit over the fireplace in the lobby. It would be the final touch to her assignment as the interior decorator for the theatre. When the artist summoned her to come to his home to view the finished painting, she was awestruck.

The majestic building, looking very much like a castle with soft clouds overhead, stood proudly in its setting. The azure blue lake at its side sparkled against the backdrop of coniferous trees of various shades of green. The artist had also captured the smallest of details: the exact tint of the mauve, blue, and white flowers that encircled the white fountains and ran aside the walkway, the paler shade of a flipped-over leaf from a willow tree, and all of the intricate shadows on the ground. When Esther saw the finished painting she was so thrilled, she had to stifle a sob when giving the artist a hug. She invited him to attend opening night and to witness the unveiling.

She'd instructed the janitor and his staff to relocate the present painting and then mount the new one, draping a cloth over it; this all had to be done quickly on opening night just before intermission, when the crowd was still in the theatre. Then, when they filled the lobby at intermission, she planned to make a short speech and unveil it. All would be happening tonight!

Oh! Jonathan and Sebastian are going to be so surprised!

She rubbed her hands together gleefully and jumped out of bed.

***

Sebastian, Esther, and I decided we would attend together. Sebastian, who agreed to drive, had the duty of being Master of Ceremonies; consequently, he wouldn't be sitting with us.

I looked through my closet and, to my delight, found a tuxedo. It was exactly what I needed to look the part of a pianist. I'd practised Beethoven's "Joyful, Joyful, We Adore Thee" over and over again until I felt it was as close to perfect as it was going to be. Oh, how excited I was to finally have the chance to perform on stage! On Earth I'd always been too busy making money to share my talent.

It was a lovely, star-lit evening. A warm breeze shimmered on the surface of the lake. The crowd came in a little at a time, and within minutes the theatre was filled to capacity. Esther and I sat in the centre row three seats up from the front, both of us filled with anticipation. I gazed around the crowd, trying to see if there was anyone in the theatre that I knew. I looked up at the balcony and there seated in the first row of the loge was the man who looked like me. I couldn't stop staring at him and decided then and there that I would make every effort to speak to him tonight, if not at intermission then definitely after the show.

I also looked around to see my grandparents. I'd delivered tickets to them, so they must be here, but where are they? Finally, I saw them directly behind me halfway up mid-centre. I turned and waved my hand in their direction and, finally, they saw me too. My grandmother blew me a kiss. I was happy knowing they were in the audience and would hear me play. I'd just started taking piano lessons when they'd left Earth.

Finally, the overhead lights were dimmed and the footlights came on. The orchestra in the pit struck up the melody "Meet Mister Callaghan" as Sebastian skipped out onto the stage with his guitar strung over his shoulder. His hair seemed a brighter red on stage against the black of his tailcoat-tuxedo. The applause was deafening. Esther and I couldn't help but nod at each other and smile.

***

Sebastian walked up to the microphone like it was familiar territory and spoke eloquently.

"Good evening, ladies and gentlemen, my name is Sebastian, and I'm delighted to be your Master of Ceremonies this evening. Welcome, welcome to the opening of our new Second Chance Theatre. We are giving singers, dancers, musicians, acrobats, poets, and comedians a second chance to come out on this brand-new stage to share their talent with you tonight.

"We have a wonderful show planned, but first I would like to introduce you to the gentlemen who have made this wonderful venue and grand evening possible: Superintendent of Construction, Alex Thompson; Landscape Specialist, John Crumpet; Musical Director, Oliver White; and the Director of tonight's show, Roland Lapierre."

As their names were called, each of the four gentlemen, clad in their best suits, proudly walked onto the stage and took a bow then formed a line, smiling to the applause before returning to their seats.

Sebastian continued, "You'll remember on Earth how each public event began with a national anthem. We cannot begin our wondrous evening without a song too. Here's one that has been especially written by a couple of my fellow angels and myself. I know you'll like it. It won't take long for you to learn the chorus. You will see the words on the overhead screen. I'll sing the chorus first so that you can learn the melody." He strummed a couple of chords then broke out in song with the uplifting melody. His deep voice resonated throughout the theatre.

"Now let's all try it!"

It was amazing how quickly the audience picked up the melody and words of the chorus. Happy voices filled the theatre. Sebastian continued singing the three verses, and the audience joined in with the chorus:

Heaven Is Where I Want To Be

Marie Rickwood

Gordon Pascoe
3min 48sec

Sebastian believed that a song is born from a thought, then the chorus and verses materialize, and finally a melody is attached. Only when it's sung publicly, and especially by a group, does it really come to life and become tangible. His heart was swelling with joy at the sound of the Second Chance Theatre's anthem coming to life so appropriately on opening night. Likewise, Jonathan and Esther couldn't stop smiling when they heard the words they had composed being sung and so musically filling the theatre.

Meanwhile, the Green Room at the back of the stage holding all of the performers was buzzing with excitement. Fresh bottles of water were provided, and joyousness hung heavy in the air as each performer waited to be called to the stage.

In the wake of the applause, Sebastian introduced the first act of the evening:

"Thank you, ladies and gentlemen. What a fine job you did with the chorus! Now I would like to tell you something about the first act we have chosen to open our show. This young lady who hails from Russia is only twelve years old, and had she stayed on Earth longer, no doubt she would have become a famous ballerina. Tonight, she will perform to the music of Tchaikovsky's *Nutcracker, Act 1, Dance of the Snowflakes.* Please welcome Anna Goroshovsky."

Clap, clap, clap!

The lights dimmed and the music slowly grew to its needed pitch. An assimilation of snowflakes barely visible fell over the stage as the footlights came on. A small, young ballerina with her dark hair in a chignon on top of her head flitted across the stage in grand leaps and pirouettes, her toes barely touching the stage. Her glittering costume in royal blue was breathtaking against the white snow, and her difficult and straining movements filled the audience with awe at how naturally she accomplished them, like a willow bending in the wind.

When the dance was over, the audience were on their feet while Anna took exaggerated bows—left, right, and centre stage. She blew kisses to the audience as she exited.

The acts that followed were equally exciting and talented and had been comprised of performers from each corner of Earth; all had missed their chance on Earth for one reason or another.

***

At intermission, the spirited audience enjoyed liquid refreshments in the large foyer, along with an assortment of snacks. A buzz of complimentary comments could be heard about the fountain, about the anthem and the performers, and how wonderful it was going to be to have this beautiful venue for their weekly entertainment. These words and more were heard amongst the bustling crowd. Many stood around the fountain beneath the atrium, while others happily gathered in little groups, all in animated conversation.

I looked for my twin in the congested crowd, but to no avail. The expectation of seeing him after the show had dimmed, but somehow I wasn't dismayed … only certain in my heart of hearts there would be an opportunity some time in the future.

***

Esther had walked out with Jonathan and Sebastian, who began mingling with the crowd. Obviously they didn't notice the covered painting over the fireplace. Jonathan spotted his grandparents and hurried over to them while Sebastian began a conversation with some members of the audience. Esther walked over to the fireplace. She reached into her pocket, extracted a whistle, and blew it three times, grabbing everyone's attention. She especially noticed the surprised look on the faces of Jonathan and Sebastian.

"Ladies and gentlemen, I'm about to unveil a painting that a very famous Earth artist painted especially for this opening. We didn't have the opportunity to meet him on Earth or see any of his original work, but tonight we will. This is, after all, Second Chance Theatre. Our Lord has told us talents are to be shared."

She broadened her smile then raised her voice. "What I am about to unveil is the work of a great artist."

She reached up to remove the veil from the painting, but alas, it was stuck and wouldn't drop down! The little hitch only added to the audience's anticipation. A tall man in the crowd came to her rescue. He reached up and gave a quick jerk, and the veil dropped. A hush fell across the audience as they stared in amazement at the beautiful painting displayed before them, then the clapping and cheers began. She heard someone ask in a voice filled with awe, "Who painted it?"

Marie E. Rickwood

painted by Michelangelo

After a few minutes, she blew her whistle again.

"Ladies and gentlemen, it is indeed my pleasure to present the painter of this beautiful work … Michelangelo!"

Amidst the multitude of gasps from the audience, he came forward, looking very much like an artist wearing a tam on the side of his head and a fresh smock over his clothes. He took a bow and received thunderous applause so rightfully deserved. People lined up to shake his hand.

Esther looked at Jonathan and Sebastian working their way through the crowd. When they caught her eye, they shook their heads in amazement. After entering the queue and complimenting and pumping Michelangelo's hand, they turned to her.

"How did you ever manage to do this? It couldn't be more appropriate," said Jonathan.

"The colours are beautiful and there's so much detail!" exclaimed Sebastian.

Before she could answer, the bell rang for the audience to return to their seats.

"I'll tell you about it later," whispered Esther as they made their way back into the theatre for the second part of the show.

***

Sebastian walked briskly out on stage.

"Ladies and gentlemen, we have with us this evening a great pianist who hails from Vancouver, Canada. Not only is he a great pianist, but also a fantastic organizer. He spearheaded the construction of this wonderful theatre we're all enjoying this evening."

"Please put your hands together for Jonathan Brown." His voice was barely heard above the thunder.

The audience rose clapping.

A grand piano was wheeled out to centre stage. The keys were gleaming white under the overhead lights. I walked out, feeling debonair indeed in my tuxedo and shiny black shoes, a spring to my step. I moved to centre stage and bowed low before taking the microphone.

"Thank you for those lovely words, Sebastian. A couple of angels helped organize the building of this Second Chance Theatre, and although they probably don't want it, they deserve recognition. Esther, please stand."

I nodded toward the front row and motioned for Esther to stand. The audience clapped loudly and whistled.

She was elegant in a long, slim-fitting gown of soft yellow. The little shrug jacket she wore glittered with sequins. Her shiny, dark hair was piled high on her head. She turned and smiled to the clapping audience.

Next I gave a sweeping gesture to the right wing, and Sebastian came out and took his bow. He appeared slightly bashful for the attention to be upon his self, but as usual wore his ready smile. Once again the applause was thunderous!

I continued, "Tonight I would like to play 'Joyful, Joyful, We Adore Thee' by Ludwig van Beethoven."

Filled with a mix of hope and excitement, I turned and walked over to the piano. I wanted so badly to play well. The intensity of my first notes hit the audience with a bang and then softness as the composition demanded. The audience was treated with the knowledge a great pianist was, without a doubt, in their midst. When the piece, so flawlessly played, was over, my bow was to a standing ovation. Although the footlights prevented me from seeing their faces, I knew they were smiling. Then I came to the full realization of how wonderful it felt to share a talent! Now I knew what I'd missed on Earth!

One act after the other performed: singers, dancers, poets, and comedians, all joyously received. The show concluded with a choir singing "Amazing Grace." Two hours after the theatre was filled, it had now emptied, yet the sound seemed to resonate from the ceiling and the walls.

The group of organizers stayed behind, discussing how delighted we all were with the success of the show. We discussed the footlights, which needed some modification—a correction to be made before next week's show.

Jonathan turned to Sebastian,

"I asked Esther how in Heaven she'd managed to get Michelangelo to create a painting for the theatre.

"I'm curious about that too," stated Sebastian.

Esther laughed. "That really has you both puzzled, hasn't it? Well, it went like this: I had to find a painter to take on the task, but it wasn't as difficult as I'd thought it would be. There are many artists of renown in Heaven, but one foremost in my mind was Michelangelo, who painted the Sistine Chapel. I'd read he was also an architect and would therefore be appreciative of the theatre's unique design. I looked up his name in Heaven's phone book and, sure enough, there he was, listed as living on Contentment Street.

"I decided it was a better idea to go directly to his home rather than phoning him first. I knew he must be elderly; I'd read he'd been of a temperamental nature on Earth, and I wasn't sure if he still painted. Those questions were quickly answered when, in response to my knock, the door opened and a smiling, elderly man stood in the doorway. He had dark brown eyes and snow-white hair. His nose appeared crooked, as though once broken. Beyond his shoulder, I saw several easels and a table loaded with paints. I thought, *Oh yes, he still paints!*

"'Hello, Michelangelo,'" I said, returning his smile. 'I've come to ask a favour of you, or should I say of your talent?'"

"'Come in, come in and have a chair,' he said.

"His voice quavered and he had a lovely Italian accent. He quickly moved some cloths and a smock from a chair so I could sit down. There was a strong smell of oil paint in the room, and I could hear opera music in the background. Then he asked me if I would like a glass of wine, saying he had some wonderful Chianti.

"I said, 'No thank you, but it's kind of you to offer.'

"Then I explained the construction of the new theatre on Rainbow Street and its main purpose of displaying and advancing talent. His eyes brightened, which made me wonder if the possibility of giving art classes in the theatre had flown into his mind.

"I told him I was hoping he would be able to paint a large image of the building, five feet high and six feet wide. I told him it would be mounted over the fireplace in the lobby and unveiled on opening night. The only problem was that it had to be accomplished very quickly. The carpenters were working on the inside of the theatre already. They expected to complete their work in about two weeks; I was afraid that didn't give him very much time.

"Michelangelo scratched his head and smiled again. 'I would consider it an honour to paint it,' he said. 'I can work quite quickly despite the age of these old bones.'

"'Wonderful!'" I said, shaking his hand. 'But how can you do it without being seen?' I asked. 'I want to surprise my friends, Jonathan and Sebastian. I've worked with them spearheading the construction of this theatre. I know they'll be delighted with the painting.'"

Esther paused and smiled at the two of us, her eyes twinkling. She had our rapt attention.

"'That's no problem,' he replied. 'I have a small covered truck. I can paint at the side of the road, and no one will know what I'm doing. I can also stretch the canvas and build the frame. Where did you say it is?'

"'At the end of Rainbow Street by the lake,' I told him."

"I'm surprised he hadn't noticed it," said Sebastian.

"I don't think he drives around very much. He told me he would start on it right away and that I should come back in ten days and he'd have it ready. Just like that. It was so easy! I shook his hand again and, when I was leaving, his voice followed me as I walked down the sidewalk.

"'La ringrazio, Esther. Hai mi ha reso molto felice oggi.'

"I'd studied the Italian language, so I understood every word," said Esther, beaming.

"What did he say?" I asked.

"In English it means, 'Thank you, Esther. You've made me very happy this day.'"

20

At Last

I bid farewell to Sebastian and Esther, telling them I wanted to walk home on this warm, moonlit night. As I strolled down Rainbow Street, I turned back to look at the theatre. It stood so proudly amongst the trees. The moon sparkled its reflection in the surface of the adjacent lake, as if to say, "Well done!"

I couldn't help giving a single clap when I turned to continue my walk, and as I admired the well-kept gardens and neatly mowed lawns, I thought about the show.

I cannot believe it—I finally played for an audience! Oh, how good it felt!

I passed the park where I'd met with my partners two weeks earlier, but something made me turn around and go back. This time, I walked through the park admiring

the shrubbery and flowers. The white flowers seemed to dazzle under the moonlight.
Then I saw him—my twin—sitting on a bench
a few yards ahead. My heart quickened and
I hurried over to him.

For me, it was like looking in a mirror:
same face, same hair, same body. The only
thing different was the clothing. My twin
wore faded blue jeans and a white shirt
with the sleeves rolled up. His shoes,
dark brown loafers, exposed white socks.

"Excuse me, I couldn't help notice how
much we look alike," I ventured.

"I am so happy to meet you, Jonathan. I
have noticed you too." His voice was soft
and crisp at the same time.

*I wonder how he knows my name. He must
have remembered it from my introduction
at the theatre.*

Momentarily we were at a loss for words,
and somehow words were not needed. My twin
was first to speak again.

"That was a magnificent show tonight.
There was much preparation put into it, I
am sure of that!"

"Yes, there was considerable planning,
but so worth it in the end. I was amazed
at what wonderful talent there is here in
Heaven, and tonight it was on display for
all to enjoy!"

"Everyone has a talent, but in a different way. Some can sing, others can dance and others, like you, Jonathan, are great managers and have a natural way of achievement."

"Thank you for the compliment. I'm curious, though, how you know my name and how are you aware of my achievements?"

"I am very pleased with the beautiful theatre and the anthem. Very pleased indeed! Gratitude is important, but too many times overlooked."

He didn't answer my question.

"How did you know my name?" I reiterated.

"Being thankful is very important," he continued. "Like grace before meals and the celebration of Thanksgiving Day, like saying thank you to others, even for little things. 'Thank' and 'you' are two beautiful little words."

"I think so too," I said. "We not only look alike, but we also think alike."

My twin smiled. A soft wind blew across the park.

"Do you think it's possible we had the same mother or father on Earth?" I asked. "I know the mother and father who raised me were my birth parents. Do you know if yours were? Perhaps the uncanny similarity between us isn't just a coincidence."

"It is truly wonderful the way some people can reach out and love a child unconditionally whether born to them or not. Love is the greatest gift of all and does not go unrewarded. Heaven's gates are open to those folks."

I thought, *He avoided my question again. I might as well play the same game and not ask him anything further that's personal. I'll just have to see where this conversation takes us. I want to see how his answers compare to those of our Lord Jesus and Esther outside the gates of Heaven.*

"When I lived on Earth, there were so many different religions professing to be the right one and the only one that would gain Heaven for its participants; this confused me and greatly contributed to my atheism. What's your opinion on that subject?"

Raising my eyebrows, I gave him my most piercing look, anxious to hear his reply.

His answer was short and succinct. "Many rivers lead to the one same ocean."

I mulled his answer over in my mind and decided there couldn't have been a better one. *Now for his opinion on the other subjects. I already have the answers but would like to hear his opinion for comparison's sake.*

"Do you think there's life on other planets besides Earth? It has been a great mystery to the people on Earth, and now I see so many people in Heaven, I'm wondering if they all came from Earth."

"I do not think it needs to be known if there are other inhabited planets. In time there may be some enlightenment, but for now there is no need for people to know the answer to this question. They are having enough trouble taking care of the Earth without having concern for another place. Creation carries the same rules, whether it be Earth or any other planet."

"Evolutionary biologists on Earth, to put it bluntly, claim man and ape share the same ancestor. What's your opinion on that subject."

"Oh that! That is a subject I like to discuss. I get a real kick out of that theory! Man was created and now this very man thinks he knows how man came to be. He claims to know more than the Creator himself. I suppose allowing a little unravelling of creation is the big tease here. I rather enjoy the scenario!"

"Why did God give mankind free will?"

"It is a precious gift, for it allows man to love with a complete heart, not because he involuntarily has to, but because he truly desires to do so."

"You must have been a philosopher on Earth. You have a strong and wise opinion on everything. I'm enjoying our conversation, I really am!

"Let's talk about all the atrocities on Earth—the wars, the greed and disregard for humanity in general. What can be done to fix those humongous problems?"

I was anxious to hear his answer.

"The answer there is so simple, I am surprised the scientists who can so eloquently expound on evolution have not realized the simple answer I am about to give you. It comes back to the little word, *love*. The school curriculum on Earth stresses many useful things, like the study of history, languages, science and all it involves, and art, to mention a few. Nowhere do we see the study of love and kindness to all. You see, it must be taught to the young, ingrained in them so that when they grow up, they can't bear to hurt anyone. We must mould the child who morphs into the adult who in turn controls the world. Simple as that. A child being trained will undoubtedly, along the way, have some influence on a parent who is not. When the next generation of parents arises, no longer will there be untrained parents."

Because his answer carried the same message as that of Jesus, I thought my twin might want to know that. I thought He also must have explained it to my twin at some given point.

"Jesus explained the very same thing to me when He met us in the restaurant."

My twin just nodded and smiled.

"I also had an in-depth lesson on Love and Kindness at my last station just outside the gates of Heaven. My friend, Esther, explained so much to me on that subject. She made me realize how wrong I'd been, made me believe, made me realize how important it is to forgive, and how Jesus made my forgiveness possible by sacrificing His life. I thanked Him for it.

"And another friend, Sebastian, helped me up the stairs when I couldn't go any farther. He was so very kind to me when I needed help. He showed how important it is to be kind to one another. I had a very long struggle making my way to the gate—and I mean a long struggle! It wasn't until I actually got there did I repent and believe in the Creator.

"Do all people have this same struggle? Did you?"

He ignored the last question.

"No, Jonathan, each is different. You needed to be prepped, ready, and brought to maximum potential, which only could be achieved by your personal struggle to become a true believer. You had to be armed and ready to help others. Who knows, there just might be a special mission ahead for you here in Heaven— one you would suit to perfection. You did such a fine job with the theatre, you may end up manning the last station, the station of Love and Kindness! I am certain the theatre can be run most efficiently by Esther and Sebastian."

This thought excited me to no end!

Another gust blew across the park, gently shaking the leaves on the trees, as though applauding the earlier decision I'd made to repent and believe. At that moment something came over me, something very special, something I didn't think was possible. I felt more elated, more gleeful than ever before! I closed my eyes, savouring the moment, then the ultimate question returned: *When will I meet the Creator?*

When I opened my eyes, my twin had vanished. I stood up, turned in every direction to scan the park, trying desperately, under moonlight, to see him, but to no avail. I turned and looked back at the bench. To my astonishment, a circle of light remained on the bench where my twin had sat.

Then a thunderbolt of realization struck me with such a force I was temporarily shaken off balance! How had something so complicated and elusive suddenly become so clear, so simple? No longer did I have to wonder and hope and dream, for at long last I had, in fact, just met God the Father, the Creator! God has indeed created us all in his image!

The End

(Or is it just the beginning?)

CPSIA information can be obtained
at www.ICGtesting.com
Printed in the USA
LVHW012357151118
597308LV00005B/5/P

9 781525 528606